'Gina's really enjoying h[...]
believe,' the Neb said wi[...]
in now and getting on very well at school.'

'That's great, Gina,' Lorelei replied, putting her arm around Gina's shoulders. 'I can't wait to meet your new friends.'

'Cool!' Paula chipped in. 'Plus we are all desperate to meet your new guy, Gina.'

'Aha!' Mrs Knebworth began, raising her eyebrows. 'You don't need to worry, Ms Winkelmann. I've met Oliver Hughes and he is a charming young man from St Lennox's. I'm sure you remember the St Lennox boys from your time at St Jude's . . . ?'

'Mrs Knebworth' – Lorelei threw an accusing look at the housemistress – 'just what is Gina getting up to over here?'

Praise for the *Secrets at St Jude's* series:

'Raucous, hilarious and heart-warming . . . from one of the UK's bestselling authors of women's fiction. Packed full of friendship, fun, entertainment, love and hope'
Lovereading

Secrets at St Jude's

Drama Girl

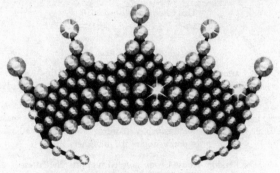

Carmen Reid

CORGI BOOKS

SECRETS AT ST JUDE'S: DRAMA GIRL
A CORGI BOOK 978 0 552 56121 1

Published in Great Britain by Corgi Books,
an imprint of Random House Children's Books
A Random House Group Company

This edition published 2010

1 3 5 7 9 10 8 6 4 2

The Random House Group Limited supports The Forest
Stewardship Council (FSC), the leading international forest
certification organisation. All our titles that are printed on
Greenpeace approved FSC certified paper carry the FSC logo.
Our paper procurement policy can be found at:
www.rbooks.co.uk/environment

Set in 12/16pt Minion

Corgi Books are published by Random House Children's Books,
61–63 Uxbridge Road, London W5 5SA

www.**kidsatrandomhouse**.co.uk
www.**rbooks**.co.uk

Addresses for companies within The Random House Group Limited
can be found at: www.randomhouse.co.uk/offices.htm

THE RANDOM HOUSE GROUP Limited Reg. No. 954009

A CIP catalogue record for this book is available from the British Library.

Printed and bound in Great Britain by
CPI Bookmarque, Croydon, CR0 4TD

MEET THE ST JUDE'S GIRLS...

GINA

Full name: Gina Louise Winklemann-Peterson

Home: A fabulous white and glass, architect-designed beach house with pool on the Californian coast

Likes: Sunshine (sadly not often found in Edinburgh), swimming, Halloween, pointy ankle boots, Prada or anything Prada-esque, Reece's Pieces, her cell phone, her little brother Menzie (sometimes), coffee, a certain charming part-time waiter at the Arts Café called Dermot O'Hagan

Dislikes: Slithery octopus-type kisses, the totally gross sludge-green St Jude's school uniform, deadly dull history lessons, Charlie Fotherington-whatsit, boiled vegetables of any kind (I mean, guys, like, haven't you heard of stir-fry?)

Would like to be: A screenwriter – but absolutely no one in the whole world knows about that

Fascinating fact: Gina has three other best friends at her old school in California – Paula, Ria and Maddison. They still can't believe she goes to boarding school in Scotland

NIFFY

Full name: Luella Edith Millicent Pethurer Nairn-Bassett (no wonder she's called either 'Niffy' or 'Lou')

Home: The ancient, crumbling, ancestral mansion Blacklough Hall in Cumbria, England

Likes: Playing pranks, enormous horses and slobbery dogs, all team games, (especially hockey – she's really good), the St J's assembly game Banshee Buzzword Bingo (which she invented), her big brother Finn, the odd sneaked glass of expensive red wine, all school food, but especially pudding

Dislikes: Dresses, dressing up, poncy shoes and fussy clothes of any description, make-up, fussing with her hair, fussing about anything at all, her real name

Would like to be: A professional rider – an international show-jumper, or maybe a three-day eventer – that way she could do show jumping, dressage and her favourite, cross-country jumping

Fascinating fact: She can be fully dressed in all her riding clothes and hat in twenty-five seconds flat

MIN

Full name: Asimina Singupta

Home: A big family house with a huge garden in a suburb of Durban, South Africa

Likes: Running really, really fast and winning, being top of the class in every single subject, doing homework (it's so interesting when you really get into it), mango lassis, gold bracelets, reading science books, borrowing Amy's clothes, her mum's home-made curries

Dislikes: The sight of blood, Biology lessons, babysitting her little brothers and sisters, the food at St J's, wearing her hair in plaits, Scottish grey skies

Would like to be: A medical researcher or medical physicist. She has to do something medical because of her doctor parents but it can't involve blood!

Fascinating fact: Min's mother taught herself Italian and went all the way to Pisa to get her medical degree

AMY

Full name: Amy Margaret McCorquodale

Home: An amazing penthouse flat in Glasgow, Scotland, with a terrace and panoramic view of the city

Likes: Designer jeans (Iceberg), designer bags (Marc Jacobs), designer boots (Jimmy Choo, but only when her dad is feeling incredibly generous), Edinburgh's Harvey Nichols (obviously), very handsome boys, diamonds, champagne, dance music, dressing up and going out, her gran's mince and tatties

Dislikes: Penny Boswell-Hackett, Mrs Norah 'the Neb' Knebworth, everything in Niffy's wardrobe, French lessons, people teasing her about her Glaswegian accent, oh and Penny Boswell-Hackett (have you got that?)

Would like to be: Officially, she's going to do a law degree, then join her dad's nightclub business. Secretly, she'd like to be a famous and fabulous actress

Fascinating fact: Amy's mum and dad were teenagers when she . . . er . . . arrived. She was brought up by her dad, her gran and her grandpa. She hasn't seen her real mum for years

Chapter One

'*Mom!*' Gina Peterson exclaimed, holding her arms wide for a hug.

She'd already galloped down the many stairs from her dorm in the St Jude's boarding house, hurtled through the long corridor and had just burst out into the entrance hall.

It had been seven whole weeks since she'd last seen her mother, and that had been back at the family home in California. It was so strange and exciting to be meeting her *here*, in Scotland, in Edinburgh, in the red and gold wallpapered entrance hall – half a world away from sunshine-soaked LA.

'Gina!' Lorelei Winkelmann exclaimed, and held out her long, slim arms in welcome. Mother and daughter hugged tightly, then let go, took a little step back and looked carefully at each other.

'You've grown – your hair looks different – and it's only been a few weeks!' Lorelei said in surprise, studying the still tanned teenager with her straight blonde hair and heart-shaped face.

'You look great,' Gina told her mom with a grin. 'How come you look so great when you've been on a plane, like, for ever?'

This was true. Lorelei's hair was pulled up into an elegant chignon; her coat, scarf and high-heeled boots all looked chic, unruffled, uncrumpled.

Somehow, Gina immediately felt too slouchy, too casual and too under-dressed – a feeling that her mother could transmit to everyone standing within a half-mile radius.

As Lorelei shrugged the compliment off, Gina's next excited question was: 'Where are Paula and Maddison? They did come, didn't they?! They are here . . . ?' She started feeling almost panicky.

Paula and Maddison were two of her best friends from California. Back when she was at regular day school in the US, these had been the girls she'd seen almost every single day – not just at school, but during the holidays, at weekends, even at night on their regular sleepovers. Along with Ria, the fourth member of the gang, these had once been her best friends in the whole world.

Now Paula and Maddison had flown all the way from California to see Gina, her new school and her new friends. Ria hadn't been able to come on this trip because her sister was in hospital.

'They're in the cab,' Gina's mother told her. 'I didn't know if it would be OK for us all to come in and look around the boarding house.'

'Of course it's OK. I'll go get them!' Gina exclaimed.

She pulled open the front door and ran down the stone steps into the driveway.

In another half-hour or so, this driveway would be full of cars as parents arrived to collect their daughters for the half-term holiday. But Lorelei was early, so right now, only a black cab was parked there, engine idling.

The two girls in the back seat were already waving frantically as Gina ran down the steps towards them.

'I can't believe it!' she called out in excitement. 'I can't believe you're here!'

The cab door swung open, and Maddison stepped out: a tall, tanned Californian teenager, complete with pink jewelled braces on her strong white teeth.

The two girls screamed in delight and ran to hug one another. Then, from the other side of the cab, Paula emerged. She was shorter, strong and wiry-looking, with walnut-brown skin and a wild mane of crinkly, all-natural, black-girl hair.

If Gina was honest, in her heart of hearts, she would say that Paula was her best friend in the whole world. She loved Maddison, Ria and the girls she'd grown so close to at St Jude's – but Paula was special. Paula had been there for her ever since kindergarten, when they'd both spent sunny mornings in the yard, teaching each other how to make the swings fly.

'I can't believe you're here!' Gina whispered into her friend's ear as they flung their arms around each other.

'Of course I'm here!' Paula told her. 'I am *dying* to see this place and meet your new friends and your boyfriend . . . Woo-hoo!' She gave a little shriek of excitement. 'He *so* better be part of our *Edinburrow* sightseeing tour, or else, Gina-wina, I am getting straight back on that plane and going home!'

'No way!' Maddison interrupted. 'At least give them time to change the in-flight movies. If I have to sit through another Anne Hathaway moment, I'm gonna die!'

'Are we coming in?' Paula asked. 'Shall I pay the fare?'

'Yeah, but Mom will pay you back,' Gina insisted. 'You're definitely coming in – I have to show you round. Plus, I think my mom is desperate to see round her old boarding house – not that it's changed much since she was here, believe me – and the girls in my dorm can't wait to meet you.'

4

'Your dorm?' Paula repeated. 'It is just so weird that you sleep in a dorm every night, Gina. I can't imagine it. So remind me: you share with Amy, Min and . . . Niffy?' she asked uncertainly.

Gina nodded. 'Yeah, they're all really, really nice. You're going to love them. C'mon!'

'Let me get my camera,' Maddison said, unzipping her handbag. Within seconds, she had her slick, silvery gadget out and was snapping Paula and Gina on the front steps of the boarding house.

'That's enough!' Gina insisted. 'Let's go in.'

As they opened the front door, they saw that Lorelei was still in the entrance hall, talking to the formidable-looking housemistress.

Mrs Knebworth, known to all the girls, behind her back, as 'the Neb', was the kind of proper, solid, more than slightly fierce woman of fifty-something who made girls nervous even when they hadn't done any-thing wrong; even when they hadn't even *thought* of doing anything wrong. It was the habit she had of fixing her steely blue eyes on you – as if she was trying to catch you out; trying, somehow, to read your guilty thoughts.

'Take a look at this place!' Lorelei exclaimed as the girls came in. 'I can't believe how well I remember it.'

'Well, we've obviously redecorated over the years,

Ms Winkelmann, but maybe always in similar shades. Feel free to take a look round. Gina, you'll be tour guide for your Californian friends, won't you?' Mrs Knebworth said in her firm, no-nonsense Edinburgh voice.

Maddison risked a reply: 'Yeah, Gina' – she nudged her friend – 'and after we see round here we want to see all round *Edinboro*. It looks so old and so way cool.'

'Quite. But it's *Edinburrrrragh*,' the Neb couldn't help correcting Maddison. She sounded as if she was clearing her throat.

Gina and Maddison exchanged a glance. Maddison's said: *Who is this strange lady?*

Gina, with a twitch of her eyebrows, hoped she was conveying: *Yes, I know, but I have to put up with her on a daily basis, so just let it go.*

'Gina's really enjoying her second term at St Jude's, I believe,' the Neb said with a satisfied smile. 'She's settled in now and getting on very well at school.'

'That's great, Gina,' Lorelei replied, putting her arm around Gina's shoulders. 'I can't wait to meet your new friends.'

'Cool!' Paula chipped in. 'Plus we are all desperate to meet your new guy, Gina.'

Oh. Good. Grief! Gina thought to herself. Did Paula *have* to mention him now? In front of the housemistress? This was about to cause a major headache.

'Aha!' Mrs Knebworth began, raising her eyebrows. 'You don't need to worry, Ms Winkelmann. I've met Oliver Hughes and he is a charming young man from St Lennox's. I'm sure you remember the St Lennox boys from your time at St Jude's . . . ?'

'Well, yes,' Lorelei began, a look of confusion on her face, 'but I thought . . .'

Gina's boyfriend was indeed charming, but he wasn't called Oliver Hughes, nor did he attend the posh and private St Lennox's. He was called Dermot O'Hagan, he went to Burnside Academy, a comprehensive, and he worked in his dad's café at the weekends – which is how Gina had got to know him.

But due to very complicated events at the Halloween party the previous night . . . Well, in a nutshell, the Neb had met Dermot but she thought he was a St Lennox boy called Oliver Hughes.

Gina had no idea how to unravel this situation. She couldn't just say: *I know his name's Oliver Hughes, but actually he prefers to be called Dermot O'Hagan – it's sort of like a nickname. And yes, I know he said he went to St Lennox's, but that was just a bit of a joke really.*

No. She didn't think that would work.

'I thought there was some boy you were seeing

called Dermot, Gina? And he works in a café?' Lorelei asked.

Gina couldn't think of anything helpful to say. She just felt a blush of meltdown proportions rushing up her face.

'Mrs Knebworth' – Lorelei threw an accusing look at the housemistress – 'just what is Gina getting up to over here?'

'A café?' the Neb spluttered.

'Can I try and explain?' Gina asked nervously.

Maddison held up her camera and took a picture of Mrs Knebworth's face. She couldn't help it – she'd never seen anyone turn purple like that before.

Chapter Two

'Oh my goodness! Look at this place!' Gina's mother kept repeating over and over again as she was led through the boarding house. 'Look at the dining room! It's just the way I remember it!' she exclaimed as she walked into the large room with its Victorian bay window and dark marble fireplace.

The long wooden tables and benches were bare – no meals were going to be served here for five days. All eighty boarders were either heading home or to friends' houses for the half-term holiday.

The Upper Fifth sitting room and the open-plan study where all the girls had a desk were both judged to be 'almost exactly the same' by Lorelei. But what really startled her was the quaint laundry and drying rooms.

'Look at those!' she cried, pointing at the ancient porcelain double sinks, all worn and cracked by the washing efforts of thousands and thousands of girls.

It had never occurred to Gina before, as she'd swirled her bras around the sinks, or hung up her wet washing in the boiler rooms fitted with ancient wooden shelves and pulleys, that this was all exactly as it had been twenty-six years ago when her own mom was at school here.

'Ooooh . . .' Maddison rolled her eyes, took a quick snap, and asked in horror, 'Do you have to wash *everything* by hand, Gina? In these old sinks?'

'No, there are washing machines too,' Gina told her.

'My goodness, Gina, how do you cope?' Lorelei wondered. 'At home Dominique does everything for you.'

'And you!' Gina retorted. 'It isn't such a big deal,' she added. 'My friends showed me what to do.'

Apparently girls who were used to maids and didn't know how to deal with their laundry were not so unusual at St Jude's.

I am the queen of washing wool, Gina remembered Niffy telling her. *Bring your jumpers to me and I will show you what to do with them. Bet you've never wrapped anything in a towel and walloped it against the floor before!*

But then Niffy could turn anything into a game or a prank or fun of one kind or another. It was her talent. Because her mother wasn't well, Niffy had missed the first half of term, but she was upstairs right now; she'd come to take Amy home with her for half term because Amy's dad was on business abroad.

'C'mon – you must have enough photos of sinks by now, Maddison,' Gina teased. 'Let's go upstairs.'

She watched as Lorelei, Maddison and Paula walked ahead of her along the corridor leading to the staircase. They seemed so bright in their Californian clothes. Maddison's jeans were lemon yellow, Paula's vivid green. Both girls wore vibrant cotton jumpers. Cotton! As if *cotton* was going to be enough to keep out the damp chill of November in Edinburgh!

Gina could almost see the boarding house through their eyes: she remembered how dark and gloomy and crustily old-fashioned it had seemed to her when she first arrived. She'd come for the summer term, all tanned and dazzled with Californian sunshine. It had taken time to adjust to the grey dampness of a Scottish May. She'd come at first because her mother, fed up with Gina's low grades and bad attitude, had made her. She'd come back this term because she'd wanted to. For Gina, St Jude's was so different, so adventurous and new – plus she really loved her new friends and hoped her old friends were going to love them too.

'Look at the stair rail!' Maddison exclaimed,

with her hand on the ornate wooden banister. 'It's sooooo old.' *Snap*. She took another picture.

'Is it always so dark up here?' Paula wanted to know as they took the staircase up and up to the second-floor bedrooms; the little ones tucked up in the attic of the cavernous Victorian house.

'Yeah, compared to back home, everything seems much darker and greyer,' Gina had to admit. 'But you get used to it. When the weather's bad, dark rooms feel cosy, I guess.'

'Cosy?' Maddison asked – she didn't think she'd heard the word before.

'Warm,' Gina explained. 'Nesty.'

'So who do you share a room with?' Lorelei asked, needing a reminder.

'OK,' Gina said, a little exasperated. 'Once again . . . try and take it in this time, Mom.'

'Sorry,' Lorelei said, 'but I'm busy. I have to remember a lot of stuff.'

But that just made it worse; that made it sound like: *I have to remember so many other things, I can't be expected to remember the names of your closest friends in Scotland.*

'There's Amy,' Gina began. 'She's really friendly and pretty, and she's from Glasgow in Scotland. She lives there with her dad – when she's not here, obviously.'

'So no mom at home?' Lorelei asked.

'No,' Gina said, and left it there. It was too soon to go into the story of how Amy's parents were teenagers when she arrived, and how her dad and her grandparents brought her up . . . Then there was the interesting fact that Amy's dad now had a boyfriend.

'Then there's Min,' Gina went on. 'She's Asian, she has this big family – four little brothers and sisters – and they all live in this huge house, close to the beach in Durban.'

'Where's that?' Maddison asked.

'South Africa.'

'An Asian girl from South Africa? That's complicated,' Paula added.

Gina smiled. 'Get used to it! There are people from all over the world here. Take me: I'm from California, but my mum's half Scottish and half German; I have a stepdad and a half-brother – that's complicated too!'

'Suppose,' Paula had to admit.

'Min's really, really nice,' Gina continued, 'and she's sooo clever. Her parents are both doctors and they want her to be a doctor too.'

Again, it seemed too soon to tell them that Min always fainted at the sight of blood and was planning on going into medical research instead.

'Then there's Niffy,' Maddison chipped in as they

took the final, narrow flight of stairs. 'I always remember her name.'

Gina told them the joke: 'She's called Niffy because her real name's Luella and she thinks it stinks. She's great. She's not been here this term – she stayed at home because her mom isn't well. Amy's going to visit with her for half-term, and then I think Niffy's coming back to school because her mom's getting better.'

By now, Gina's hand was on the doorknob of her dorm. She looked at the faces of the three people who'd travelled all this way to see her, her new school and her new friends. It was kind of exciting to get these two groups of people together.

Pushing open the door, she announced: '*Ta-dah.*'

'Hi!'

'Come on in . . .'

'Welcome to the Iris dorm,' the voices inside the room chorused.

The Californians squeezed themselves through into the cramped room.

Three beds, three chests of drawers and a wardrobe had been shoe-horned into the room, leaving hardly any floor space for anything else. If Niffy was coming back after half-term, a bunk bed would have to be installed.

Maddison's camera flashed several times, making the dorm girls blink with surprise.

'Whoa!' Amy said, and held her hand up in front of her face. She hated having her photo taken – well, unless she'd spent hours arranging her hair and make-up beforehand.

Hurried, last-minute packing was in progress: Amy's suitcase was wide open on her bed as she tried to decide which of her many wonderful outfits should come with her to Niffy's threadbare ancestral home, Blacklough Hall.

Lorelei, Maddison and Ria shook hands with everyone and said friendly hellos.

'What lovely clothes!' Paula exclaimed as she cast a practised eye over the expensive jeans, cute tops and label-laden little skirts Amy had spread out over her bed.

'Thanks!' Amy replied. 'Gina says there are some great shops in California. I must come and visit some time.'

'Definitely!' Gina said, thrilled at the idea.

Lorelei was shaking Niffy's hand. She wouldn't be shaking it quite so hard, or smiling in quite such a friendly way, thought Gina, if she knew that this was the girl who'd helped Gina break into the school records office last term to find out all about her mother's time at St Jude's.

'Hi, Ms Winkelmann, it's so nice to finally meet you,' Amy gushed. 'I'm sorry about the mess in here. It's just, I'm going to Niffy's place – the coldest house in the known universe – so I have to take a lot of clothes.'

'Not that *that's* going to keep you very warm,' Niffy pointed out, picking up a vibrant pink mini-dress and holding it against her tall, long-limbed frame.

'It's a layer,' Amy insisted. 'Aren't you supposed to wear lots of layers in sub-zero temperatures?'

'It's not that bad at Blacklough!' Niffy protested.

Amy looked up, caught Gina's eye and gave a little laugh. 'Yes it is! It is pure, dead frrrrreezing!' she insisted, rolling her rs for effect. 'Back me up here – Gina? Min?'

'It is quite cold, yes, I would have to agree, but maybe because we're not used to it. We're not out-doorsy types like you, Niffy,' Min said diplomatically, brushing through her waist-length hair and preparing to tie it in a plait for her auntie's approval.

'I have loads and loads of jumpers at home, plus jackets and coats, so you don't need to worry,' Niffy said, earning herself a roll of Amy's eyes.

Amy was a strictly designer-label girl. She was only fifteen but she already had account cards for all the smartest shops in both Edinburgh and her home town, Glasgow. Her jeans, her tops, her jackets, her dresses, her shoes, her handbags – in fact just about every single item she owned, apart from her school uniform – had an impressive, expensive label attached. The idea of allowing one of Niffy's great hairy, smelly, horsy jumpers or vile, damp wax jackets to even come in contact with her was just . . . Ugh! Enough to make her shudder.

'What are your plans for half term?' Min asked, politely turning to the visitors.

'Well, we're going to stay in Edinburgh for a couple of days,' Lorelei replied. 'Do some sightseeing and some shopping. Then we're going to make a trip to one of the little islands off the West Coast.'

'Very nice,' Amy said. 'So, you must be Maddison?' she asked, looking at Paula.

'No!' Paula seemed slightly taken aback. 'I'm Paula, this is Maddison. People don't usually confuse us – it's not like we look the same. I mean, she's blonde and I'm black!'

'Sorry,' Amy said. 'And you were both at school with Gina back in the States?'

'Yeah, Gina and I have known each other since kindergarten. Hasn't she told you all about us?' Paula asked, sounding hurt. 'Because there's nothing about Gina that we can't tell you. We just heard all about your Halloween party and Dermot sneaking in under the name of Oliver Hughes – your house-mistress wasn't too pleased to find out about that.'

'I think Halloween's a bigger deal in the States though,' Maddison chipped in. 'We were so sorry to miss our school's party this year. Everyone dresses up—'

'Everyone dressed up for our party,' Amy pointed out.

'Yeah, but we have these amazing carved pumpkins all the way up the road to the school—'

'We had pumpkin lanterns on the boarding-house steps—' Niffy countered.

'And we have all this Halloween candy – mountains of it – and people make pumpkin pie and it's a really big deal.' Maddison was determined to make her point.

'Bet you didn't have liquorice treats shaped like real beetles,' Niffy added.

'Oh, they were invented in the States years ago,' came the breezy reply.

'I thought *three* of your friends were coming over?' Niffy said to Gina.

'Ria couldn't come,' Paula answered. 'Her sister is sick. An ED – it's serious, so Ria doesn't want to leave her family right now. Didn't Gina tell you?'

Although Niffy, Amy and Min would have liked to ask what an ED was, the pleased look on Paula's face, the happy 'I-know-something-you-don't-know' expression put them off.

It also inspired Amy to enquire, 'Have you heard about the play Gina's written? It's going to be performed at school later this term.'

'No,' Lorelei replied. 'Gina, how fantastic! You should have told us—'

'I thought I had – I know I meant to,' Gina added quickly. She didn't want anyone to feel left out or hurt.

'We've known all about the play for weeks,' Amy said. Then, sneakily, she added, 'It's called *Seeing Scarlett*, and it's based on something that happened to Gina.'

'Really?' Lorelei wasn't the only one who looked surprised to have heard nothing about this.

But Paula quickly countered, 'Of course, we know that Gina's a really good writer. We've known her for sooooo long – we learned to read and write together. We've been at swim camp together every summer since we were—'

'Ten,' Maddison was quick to point out.

'That's nice,' Amy said coolly. 'But I feel I've got to know Gina really well too, and because we're together all day and every weekend—'

'We have a great time together,' Niffy chipped in. 'I suppose that's why you decided to stay on, Gina. You were only supposed to come to St Jude's for a term, weren't you?'

There was an awkward silence before Lorelei replied, 'I was very pleased with how well Gina was getting on at school here – but, yes, Gina's the one who wanted to come back.'

'There are so many things I miss about California though, especially you guys,' Gina quickly told Maddison and Paula. 'It's so amazing you've come over!'

She hoped this would ease the growing sense of tension in the room. Why were her friends all trying to prove they knew her the best?

'Gina, are you going to let your mum and your friends meet Dermot?' Amy underlined that she was Gina's really good friend, who knew all about Dermot.

'Oh, I hope so.' Paula turned to Gina with a smile. 'We've heard so much about Dermot – haven't we, Maddison?'

'Well . . . we'll see,' Lorelei answered. She caught Gina's eye and gave her a slightly disapproving look.

'Dermot's lovely,' Niffy told them.

'We *have* to meet him,' Maddison pleaded. 'C'mon, Ms Winkelmann. We've got to get to know Gina's guy!'

'I'm not sure if we're going to have time for that. I have a pretty big schedule planned,' Lorelei replied. 'Are you all packed up to come to the hotel with us, Gina?'

'That would be such a shame,' Amy couldn't resist adding. 'You won't get to know him as well as we do.'

'We *have* to!' Maddison insisted.

Gina felt as if she was being pushed and pulled from one side of the room to the other: the Californians on one side, the Iris dorm girls on the other. She was in a tug of war between them.

Stop it! she wanted to shout out. She liked all these girls. No, she *loved* them. They had to stop this point-scoring about who knew her best.

'Ms W,' Paula began firmly, 'if you don't let us meet Dermot, we're not setting foot on the boat that's going to take us out to your cute little island.'

Chapter Three

Once Gina was in the taxi, she found she was able to focus much better on her mother and the two friends who'd all made such a long journey to see her.

As the grey stone terraces of Georgian Edinburgh whizzed by, she was no longer worrying about whether Niffy's mum was going to be OK, or if Amy was going to be warm enough at Blacklough Hall, or if Min was going to survive an entire half term at her auntie's in Leicester – *the most boring family I've ever met, trust me.*

No, now she found herself slipping back into Californian Gina. Her accent seemed to grow stronger and more twangy with every word, and suddenly she wanted to know all about what was going on back home.

How was her brother, Menzie? How was Mick, her stepdad? What was all the latest news from her old school?

'You will never guess who Ria is seeing now...' Maddison was telling her, and Gina found herself dying to know.

'Lewis Bayer! Do you remember him?' Maddison revealed.

'Of course! Of course I remember him. No way!' Gina replied. 'And what's her sister got? What's an ED?' she asked.

'An eating disorder,' Paula told her. 'Megan's really underweight and really sick. They won't let her out of the hospital until she weighs more.'

'Oh my goodness! How awful.' Gina resolved to call Ria just as soon as she could.

Lorelei wasn't saying anything, but she was listening, which struck Gina as unusual. Normally her mom could always find something else to be doing. She hated to sit still, to 'waste time'. Sitting down just to talk wasn't something she did often.

But here she was with her head turned towards them, listening. Her brand-new BlackBerry phone – so she could keep in touch with everything going on back at the office – was in her handbag, not in her hands.

Ah . . . but of course! Gina realized. It was still the small hours of the morning in California, so even Lorelei probably didn't have any mail in her inbox just yet.

'I suppose you'd better give Dermot a call then,' Lorelei said all of a sudden, making Gina start.

'Wha . . . ?' she began.

'Yeah.' Lorelei smiled encouragingly. 'Not just because of Paula's threats. If he's important to you, then I'd like to meet him.'

Paula and Maddison began to whoop and whistle their encouragement.

'Well, I guess . . . I mean . . . I can try . . .' Gina offered shyly. 'Not here,' she added quickly. 'Not in front of you guys!'

'Here's our hotel,' Lorelei said, glancing out of the window just as the taxi swooped into the entrance driveway.

Before she'd even stepped out of the cab, Gina could see that it was a gorgeous hotel – but then she had expected nothing less. Her mother and stepfather worked very hard running their own software company. As a result of their efforts they were unmistakably rich. Home in California was a wonderful modern mansion with huge plate-glass windows, marble floors, a full-sized pool and staff. Obviously Lorelei wasn't going to slum it when she went on holiday. In fact, she liked to live even more luxuriously whenever they went away. So Gina knew this big, imposing building was going to be a full-on five-star residence with all the trimmings.

Through the glittering entrance hall they went, and into a shiny lift where a doorman in top hat and tails pressed the button for them.

On the first floor, at the end of a plushly carpeted corridor, they found their rooms.

'Wow!' Gina gasped, as she opened the door. It wasn't just the chandeliers or the three generous beds draped with velvet and satin; it was the stunning view out over the rooftops of Edinburgh.

She loved the shiny slate roofs, the crooked chimney pots and higgledy-piggledy rows of houses stretching all the way out to the imposing set of hills which framed the city in the distance. She loved the fact that people had been standing in rooms like this looking out at this view for hundreds of years. Sure, there had been a few changes here and there, but this town was so old, it humbled you.

'The girls' dorm,' Lorelei explained. 'Is that going to be OK?'

'Yeah!' all three friends agreed.

'I'll be next door,' she told them. 'There might be some work I'll need to catch up with late at night. I have a new personal assistant and I don't know if she's shaping up as well as I'd hoped.'

'Thanks, Mom,' Gina said. She'd thought maybe

she'd be sharing with her mother, but she was pleased Lorelei had understood that this arrangement was going to work much better. She, Paula and Maddison had so much late-night catching up of their own to do.

'So what are we going to do today?' Gina wondered out loud as she set her bag down on the thick blue carpet.

Lorelei checked her small, diamond-studded watch. 'It's a full day of sightseeing, baby,' she replied. 'Paula and Maddison are only in Edinburgh for two days, so we have to show them all the best things. I've got tickets booked for the castle at two thirty.'

How could Gina have thought for a moment that her mother wouldn't have a plan?

'Gee! It is soooo old. It is soooo historical. I can't believe how *old* it is!' Maddison gushed all over again.

They'd walked up the long, cobbled Royal Mile leading to the gates of Edinburgh Castle. Perched high above the city, the castle walls gave a panoramic view over Edinburgh and the surrounding countryside.

Even in the slanting golden sun of a Scottish afternoon, the light seemed to be fading fast. Although it was the first of November, the castle was packed with tourists.

Gina had never been in this part of the town before.

Her school friends had always laughed at the idea of going to the castle because it was 'so touristy'. Now, although she was acting the part of tour guide, she felt just as bowled over by it all as the others.

On each side of the street leading to the castle, shops were selling the Scottish paraphernalia that Scots themselves never seemed to eat, wear or use: shortbread, crystal tumblers, walking sticks made from antlers, ceremonial swords, shields with clan crests emblazoned on them.

Paula and Maddison couldn't get enough of the tourist shops and kept flitting in and out of them, while Gina and her mom stood outside, giggling and rolling their eyes at each other.

Before they'd even got to the castle, Paula had bought a miniature ceremonial sword and a cuddly Highland cow, while Maddison had been unable to resist red cashmere gloves and a crystal paperweight in the shape of a Scottie dog.

'Isn't he adorable?' she asked, taking the dog out of the tartan (of course) paper bag he'd been wrapped in.

'Erm . . .' For a moment Gina wasn't quite sure what to say, but then she teased, 'I think you might have jet lag – your sense of taste hasn't caught up with British time yet.'

Once they were inside the castle grounds, they all

became just as excited as all the other tourists. They had their photos taken beside Mons Meg – the huge cannon. They gazed and 'gee whizzed' at the tiny chapel, and looked up in amazement at the mighty wooden roof of the great hall.

'Look at the size of that fireplace – you could burn people alive in there. D'you think that's what they did?' Maddison wondered out loud.

The dungeon prisons were genuinely spooky, decked out with hammocks and flickering flames. The dark stone walls rang with the shouts and cries of recorded voices begging for help, mercy and forgiveness.

Gina read the information boards on the walls. 'American prisoners were kept here,' she told the others, 'during the War of Independence.'

Paula and Lorelei came to stand beside her. '*They were seen as traitors,*' Lorelei read aloud, '*held without trial, often for years, on the other side of the world from their homes* . . . Good grief. We're in the Guantanamo Bay of the seventeen hundreds.'

Suddenly her phone began to bleep and her attention was diverted.

'Offices will soon be opening for business on the West Coast,' Gina told Paula.

'Never mind that – this is so awesome!' Paula

whispered back. 'Look at this wooden door: it has graffiti on it dating from seventeen twenty-three!'

'Paula, if you or Maddison say "awesome", "historic", "quaint" or "sooooo old" just one more time, I'm going to kill you!' Gina warned. 'There will be no mercy – I'm just going to jump up and kill you!'

The mobile in Gina's pocket began to ring, and suddenly she felt shy. There was only one person this could be. She'd texted and left voicemail for Dermot; now, it seemed, he was calling her back.

She walked down the corridor, turning away from her mom and her friends for a little privacy.

'Hi?' she answered the call.

'Hiya!'

Oh! That single word was full of Dermot's warm, friendly smile.

'How are you?' she asked.

'I'm fine – a little bruised and sore after last night, and I'm not sure that the Shrek costume will ever look the same again – but hey, I'm fine,' he said, referring to the Halloween adventures of the night before. 'How are you? Are you surrounded by gorgeous Californians?'

'Yeah, who think Edinburgh is *sooooo quaint* and old and, like, *really, you know, historic*!' she joked.

'You were never, ever like that, of course,' Dermot teased.

'I wasn't!' Gina insisted.

'So . . . you want me to come and meet your friends and your scary *mom* and have dinner with you tonight?' Dermot had just listened to the request on his voicemail.

'Yeah,' Gina confirmed. 'What do you think of that idea?'

'I think it's terrifying!' Dermot admitted. 'I'd rather be boiled in hot oil than meet your mom for dinner. I mean, isn't she the head of Global Mega Software Bigwigs or something? And you know what my table manners are like.'

'They're fine!' Gina reassured him. 'You'll be fine. She'll love you.'

This made Dermot laugh. 'Gina, there is no mother in the world who likes the boy her fifteen-year-old daughter is dating,' he informed her. 'I know this because my mum told me.'

'So it must be true. But your mum quite liked me, didn't she?'

'Ah, yeah, but that's different. You are a girl, I'm a boy. You are a civilizing influence . . . apparently.'

'Cute!'

'I've got a better idea,' Dermot said. 'Do you know about the ghost tours they do at night?'

'No!' Gina answered. *Ghost tours? At night?* This sounded a little crazy: typically Dermot.

'Yeah, nine p.m. You, your mom and your friends meet me at Milne Close, just off the Royal Mile, and we'll go on a guided tour of Edinburgh's darkest and spookiest places. That way, your mom is distracted and can't concentrate on all my bad points too hard. Plus, I'm able to hold your hand without looking too suspicious.'

'Because I'll be scared?' Gina said with a laugh. 'Of some stupid ghost tour?'

'Go on,' Dermot said as persuasively as he could. 'It'll be fun. Dinner scares me much more than ghosts.'

'Well . . . I'll have to ask Mom. And remember, Dermot, when you meet her, be neat, do not be late – she really doesn't do late – and *please*, don't try and be funny,' Gina warned him. 'She doesn't do jokes.'

'OK, no jokes, no jokes,' he repeated. 'I'll get that tattooed onto my forehead to remind me.'

As soon as Gina was off the phone, Lorelei informed her that Paula and Maddison wanted to go back to the hotel for a nap once the castle tour was over.

Gina couldn't help feeling disappointed. They had

the whole of Edinburgh to explore! So many things to see and do, and so little time left already. Why did they want to go back to the hotel and sleep?

'No! No sleeping yet!' Gina complained. She turned to her friends, but now that she looked at them properly, she could see that they were exhausted.

'We've been awake all night, Gina,' Paula reminded her. 'Unlike your mom, we need sleep! Look, we're planning a nap and then we'll join you and Dermot' – this came with a wink – 'for dinner.'

'He doesn't want to do dinner,' Gina said, now that she had everyone's attention.

'Oh?' Lorelei looked at Gina with surprise.

'He's suggested meeting up later tonight for a ghost tour.'

'A ghost tour? Cool!' Paula said immediately.

Maddison nodded, but Lorelei took a little longer to make up her mind. 'Tonight? Instead of dinner?' she looked uncertain.

'Please, Mom,' Gina wheedled.

'Well . . . maybe it could be fun . . .' Lorelei said doubtfully. 'You girls will have had a rest . . . OK. OK, we'll do it, but only if you come shopping with me while Paula and Maddison are sleeping.'

'Oooooooh, yeah!' Gina agreed immediately. It had been too long since she'd hit some really nice shops with her mom – and, most importantly, her mom's purse – to accompany her.

Lorelei looked up from the email she was tapping out on the little screen in her hands and glanced at her daughter, who was stepping out of the changing room.

'That is gorgeous – you have to have it!' she told Gina; then her eyes were drawn back down to the phone screen once again.

'But it's white!' Gina protested, and surveyed herself carefully in the mirror. She wasn't sure.

'It's ivory,' her mother countered. 'Gina, I'm sorry but you look adorable!'

The dress was undeniably cute. It was neat and fitted, tailored almost. It stopped well above the knee and had silky sleeves that draped down past her elbow and ended in a graceful cuff. It was so elegant – but maybe just ever so slightly grown up.

Gina wondered when she would have the chance to wear it. Was this the kind of thing she could wear at the Christmas ball? Or should she be buying a proper ball gown?

She wasn't sure . . . But even if it wasn't a ball gown, this little white number was lovely.

Gina looked at herself closely in the mirror: the pale colour set off her long golden hair and her still tanned arms and face. She thought about Amy, fashion leader of the dorm, and imagined the rapturous reception the dress would earn from her. Amy would probably bribe her to borrow this.

Lorelei tucked away her phone and turned to give Gina her full attention. 'Sorry – there's a big deal coming up,' she explained.

Gina was tempted to say, *Isn't there always?* but she bit her tongue. She had her mother's attention now, didn't she? She shouldn't complain.

'That dress would look so great with boots,' Lorelei coaxed. 'C'mon, shall we go take a look-see in their shoe department?'

Gina shot her mom a smile. 'Yeah, but just remember this was all your idea,' she replied.

Once the ivory dress and a pair of unbelievably sweet pale patent-leather boots had been wrapped up and passed painlessly over the cash desk, Lorelei couldn't resist trying on a few things she'd spotted for herself.

As she came out of the changing room in a glamorous jacket, she asked Gina, 'So, are we going to meet your boyfriend tonight? Have you said yes to the ghost thing yet?'

'Do you definitely want to do it?' Gina asked. 'I just wanted to check with you again.'

'Are we going on the ghost tour because he's scared of having dinner with me?' her mom wondered.

'Um . . . maybe a little,' Gina admitted, feeling slightly embarrassed about this line of questioning. 'You have to admit, you can be quite scary.'

'You really like him, don't you?' Lorelei asked next.

Now Gina could feel the tingle of a blush spread from her neck up and over her cheeks. 'Mom!' she protested.

'It's OK!' Lorelei was smiling. 'It's allowed. You can have a boyfriend, Gina – and you know what? I don't even have to like him. It's not like you're getting married or something!'

'*Mom!*' Gina was horrified. 'If you say anything like that – if you even think of making a joke about that . . . I will kill you!'

'Call him!' Lorelei instructed with a twinkle in her eye. 'Say we'll be there.'

Chapter Four

Amy watched as rain lashed down on the windscreen of the old Range Rover. Worn, battered wiper blades scraped across the glass, barely removing enough water for Niffy's dad, Mr Nairn-Bassett, to be able to see the small twisting road from Berwick-upon-Tweed station to the Nairn-Bassett family home, Blacklough Hall.

'Welcome to the Wet Country, where the rain never stops falling,' Niffy announced from her seat in the back beside Amy. 'Hope you brought your canoe, Amy. We might have to paddle the rest of the way.'

Not for the first time it occurred to Amy that she liked Niffy almost as much as she hated Blacklough. There was certainly no one else in the world who would be able to persuade her to keep coming down here – to this damp green patch of boring countryside, where there was nothing to do except walk in the rain, ride in the rain, bike in the rain, get wet in the rain, sneeze in the rain, blow your nose in the rain . . . and so on.

Blacklough Hall was the most decrepit, run-down, dusty, freezing, stately hell-hole that Amy had ever encountered. It was certainly nothing like her home, that was for sure. Amy was the only daughter of a very successful Glaswegian nightclub owner, and home was a luxurious penthouse flat – her dad had grown up in a tower block and liked a big view.

Amy's idea of a wet room was a luxury power-shower; Niffy's idea of a wet room was one with buckets on the floor to catch the leaks from the roof. Amy's idea of a takeaway was a gorgeous curry shared with her dad on the plush sofa in front of a film. Niffy's takeaway food was the stuff found growing amongst the weeds in the Blacklough garden: black-berries, parsley, the odd spear of asparagus or stick of rhubarb.

These people owned a house the size of a museum, but because they spent all of their tiny income sending their kids to boarding school, they didn't have a penny to repair the place or even heat it.

'Why don't they sell it and live somewhere normal – somewhere warm and dry?' Amy had asked Niffy countless times before.

'Sell it? Are you mad!' Niffy would answer. 'That

house has been in the Nairn-Bassett family for eight generations. My dad isn't going to be the one to let it go.'

'Maybe you will though,' Amy had speculated. 'Maybe you'll be the one who sees sense?'

'Maybe I'll become a world-famous show-jumper, earn multi-millions and be able to fix it up – put in central heating and re-do the roof.'

'Hmm . . . maybe,' Amy had said doubtfully.

'How's Mrs Nairn-Bassett?' Amy asked Niffy's dad now, although Niffy had already told her that Mrs N-B, who'd been diagnosed with leukaemia in the summer, was showing the first signs of recovery.

'She's getting on very well, thank you for asking,' came Mr N-B's reply. He sounded stiff, formal and painfully polite. To deflect any further questions, he immediately asked, 'And how's your father?'

'He's good. He had to go over to the States this week; otherwise I wouldn't be here – obviously . . . thanks for having me, anyway.'

'Oh, no bother, no bother at all. Great company for Lou and Finn.'

Lou was Niffy. Niffy's real name was Luella, but everyone who didn't know her as Niffy called her Lou. It was very confusing.

Amy's name situation was very simple: everybody

called her Amy – well, except, OK, sometimes Niffy was allowed to call her 'Aim'.

'Finn's here already, isn't he?' Niffy asked her dad.

'Yes, got in this morning,' Mr N-B replied.

'Great!' Niffy said with enthusiasm. 'It's been ages since I've seen him.'

Amy, an only child, wondered if sisters were usually this keen to see their older brothers. She'd met Finn many times and thought he was OK, in a lanky, boyish kind of way, but she understood that he and Niffy were close – probably because they had to stick together in the craziness of the N-B family home.

'Any plans for the holiday?' Mr N-B asked the girls.

'We're going to spend one day in town and go to the new swimming pool there,' Niffy replied.

'Excellent!' Mr N-B approved.

The car turned off the country road and up the drive of Blacklough Hall. Within moments, the imposing grey stone building was looming in front of them.

It looked even saggier and shabbier than Amy remembered. Green moss was growing over the stonework and greying paint was peeling from every one of the small-paned windows. Rainwater gushing out of cracked gutters ran unchecked into large damp patches on the walls.

Amy could just imagine the buckets that would be set out in the attic rooms where she and Niffy would be sleeping tonight. *Plink, plonk,* the water would drip through the roof into the buckets all night long, keeping her awake.

The car drove past the front of the house and round to the back door. This way they would enter the house through the only warm room – the kitchen – where Mrs N-B was bound to be putting something fairly disgusting together for dinner.

Amy took her bag out of the car, hoisted it up onto her shoulder and stepped carefully over the mud and gravel in boots too high-heeled and too pointy for the countryside. She entered the narrow, dark corridor, and was greeted enthusiastically by two massive, furry, smelly dogs: Doughal and Macduff.

'Down, boys, *down*!' Niffy commanded, but not before one of them had licked Amy right across the face with a great damp, stinky tongue.

'Euuurrrgh!' she protested. For a moment she thought she was going to be sick. The dog's wet saliva was all over her cheeks and she could smell it!

'Amy!' Wiry little Mrs N-B was hurrying towards her now, and before Amy could do anything about it, she'd kissed Amy on both cheeks, pressing her lips right into the dog spit.

'I'm sorry . . .' Amy pulled away. 'The dog licked me
– I've not had a chance to—'

'Oh dear me,' Mrs N-B said, wiping at her own lips
now as Amy took a crumpled tissue out of her pocket
and rubbed over her cheeks hard.

'I think I'll go and wash my face,' she said.

'Yes, of course. Niffy will help you take your bag up.
You're in the same room as last time – I hope that's
OK.'

Plink, plonk, plink, plink, plonk . . . The rain orches-
tra started up in Amy's head. But she replied cheerily,
'Lovely, thanks. Thank you for inviting me.'

Mrs N-B smiled at her. 'Oh, it'll be fun to have you,
Amy. Don't mention it.'

As Amy passed the ancient old Aga cooker, she saw
the vast pot of green soup bubbling ominously on
the hob. Oh, good grief! It was probably made
out of nettles picked from the garden or something
awful.

Why had she come here? *Why?* She could have
stayed with a day-girl friend and be having a perfectly
civilized time in Edinburgh, instead of battling the
elements, the dodgy food and the crazy Nairn-Bassetts
for the next five days.

Niffy led the way along one dingy corridor and into
another, and they took the creaky wooden back stairs

up two flights to the attic rooms at the top of the house.

With each step, Amy was feeling grumpier and grumpier. Dog slobber was drying on her face, and she would be standing in a field in the rain watching Niffy ride for the rest of the week. What on earth was she going to do for fun around here?

They went past the little room stuffed with old sofas and an ancient TV, still affectionately known as 'the playroom'. The TV was on and the door was open just wide enough for Amy to be able to see the back of a sofa and the dark hair of the TV viewer.

'Hey, Fin-Fin!' Niffy called out, and pushed open the playroom door.

The head on the sofa turned. A wide grin split the face that was now turned in their direction.

'Hello!' Finn called out, and bounded up off the sofa to greet them. 'Lou!' he said fondly, treating his sister to a huge bear hug.

Then he let go of Niffy and turned to Amy. 'Hello, Amy, it feels like ages,' he said with a smile, and held out his hand for her to shake.

As she took hold of it, Amy could feel more of a grin than she'd intended spreading across her face. 'Hi, Finn,' she said, meeting the fun-filled brown eyes under the dark, arching eyebrows that gave a questioning look to his smile.

Finn was about six inches taller than the last time she'd seen him: he was thin but broad-shouldered – he'd definitely filled out a bit. His hair was a glossy dark brown, casually floppy, and he was so, *so* much better looking than Amy remembered.

It occurred to her that they'd been shaking hands and checking each other out for just a little bit too long now. Could it be that he was looking at her the way she was looking at him? With interest; with real, feeling-stirring interest?

Suddenly the prospect of a half term at Blacklough Hall didn't seem so bad after all – now that she knew Niffy's brother was going to be here.

Chapter Five

It was very cold in Milne Close at two minutes to nine that evening. At least Gina was wearing a proper feather-filled duvet coat and a furry hat – she knew just how brutal the Edinburgh weather could be. But she felt very sorry for Paula and Maddison, who were hopping from foot to foot, pulling their thin anoraks tightly around them to try and keep out the biting night air.

Lorelei looked as elegant as ever, with her collar turned up and her chic coat belted against the chill. 'He's late,' she pointed out, as if Gina somehow hadn't noticed that Dermot wasn't here yet.

'Well . . . it's not quite nine yet. Maybe he's been held up,' Gina offered.

'At nine we set off. That's when the tour begins. We can't keep the guide and the rest of the group waiting!' Lorelei already sounded snappy. As Gina had warned Dermot, she hated unpunctuality. This wasn't exactly a great start for him.

Gina hadn't expected the tour to be quite so busy. There were about thirty other tourists milling about the pavement with tickets, brochures and street maps in their hands, chatting in many different languages. Gina recognized the word for 'cold' in both French and Spanish.

'Right . . . is that us then?' asked the guide, a middle-aged man bundled up in a thick woollen over-coat and scarf.

Lorelei looked at Gina and shrugged. 'Have you tried to call him?' she asked her.

'What do you think?' Gina snapped back.

Then she got a nudge in the ribs from Paula as Maddison pointed at a figure racing along the pave-ment towards them.

'Is that him?' Paula asked.

'Yes!' Gina answered, able to tell at once.

She recognized Dermot's battered old coat, which she knew he'd bought in a charity shop; she recog-nized his military short haircut, which he was growing out just for her – and, well, because his mum preferred it longer too. Most of all, as he drew closer, she recognized his broad grin.

'I'm sorry! I am *so* sorry!' Dermot announced as soon as he'd spotted them and was within reach. 'My bus . . .' he went on, panting with the effort of the long uphill sprint. 'It didn't come for hours! I was beginning to think it would never come . . . had been abducted by aliens or something.' He smoothed his hair down nervously and smiled at Gina.

'OK, everybody ready?' the guide asked. 'Do you have a ticket?' he asked Dermot.

While Dermot was patting down his coat in search of his wallet, Lorelei held up the five tickets she'd bought, and told the guide, 'He's covered.'

'Very well, follow me,' he instructed.

As the thirty or so tourists fell in behind him, Dermot started on a round of handshaking.

Nervously he turned first to Gina's mom. 'Ms Winkelmann, how are you? Very nice to meet you . . . Obviously I'm late, you've had to buy my ticket and I've made a terrible first impression. I will totally understand if you want me to just leave now and never contact your daughter again . . .'

Gina gave Dermot a nudge, hoping he would remember her instruction about not being funny. While she loved Dermot's ability to turn just about everything into a joke, she didn't think her mom would get it.

Paula and Maddison giggled nervously. They hadn't come across Dermot's brand of humour before, but they too realized it might not appeal to Lorelei.

'No, Dermot,' Lorelei said, taking hold of his hand and shaking it briefly, 'I don't think that will be necessary.' She gave a small smile before adding, 'Gina tells me that you're very amusing,' but the way she said this implied that she disagreed.

'Gina is a very kind and generous person,' Dermot offered.

'Hmmm . . . Anyway, this is Paula.' Lorelei made the introduction.

'Paula, yes, I guessed it was you – Gina's told me all about you,' Dermot said, winning himself an instant friend. 'And Maddison, isn't it? Hi. Welcome to the balmy warmth of Edinburgh in November. Gina? Yes' – he risked giving her a small peck on her cheek – 'I think we've met before, haven't we?'

She smacked his arm playfully. 'Look at your eye!' she exclaimed, seeing the purplish bruise and crusty scab on the side of Dermot's face properly for the first time.

'Yeah, well, nothing serious – healing up nicely,' he insisted.

They had both had quite an adventure at the party the night before – what with a prowler, an Internet stalker and several Halloween pranks.

'Did this happen last night?' Lorelei asked. 'Gina has done some explaining, but I don't think Mrs

Knebworth is very pleased that you got in under false pretences.'

'Erm . . . no . . .' Dermot agreed, realizing this was awkward.

'You should probably go round there and offer her an apology,' Lorelei suggested.

Dermot and Gina exchanged glances. Go round and apologize? To Norah the terrifying Neb?

'You're right,' Dermot began. 'And hopefully I'll live, you know, to tell the tale.'

Instead of laughing, Lorelei made an unamused throat-clearing kind of sound. Fortunately the tour had now come to a halt in front of the cathedral, and the guide turned to face them.

The tourists fell into respectful silence and the Americans and Dermot had to do likewise.

The guide began to tell them about ghosts. After several minutes Gina realized that it certainly wasn't the most thrilling talk she had ever heard.

'I think this is going to be cold and boring,' she whispered to Dermot.

He pushed his hand into her coat pocket and squeezed her cold fingers. 'Trust me, at the end of the Royal Mile he takes us to one of the oldest houses in Edinburgh and that's when it gets properly scary.'

Gina smiled and raised her eyebrows at him.

'Seriously!' he promised. 'And he's good.' He tilted his head towards the tour guide. 'He just needs to warm up.'

'Me too. So you take a lot of girls on the ghost tour, do you?' Gina couldn't help asking.

'No!' Dermot replied, before being shushed by a Spaniard with threateningly bushy eyebrows.

The blackened stone house at the end of the Royal Mile was very old. It had a gnarled front door decorated with hundreds of years worth of scrapes and scratches. Great metal hinges anchored it to the stone walls and it was locked with two rusting iron bolts.

The guide wrestled the bolts back and then took a key out of his pocket; it was several centimetres long and intricately wrought.

'Now, this house has no less than seven ghosts all of its own. All seven have been independently witnessed many times,' he said in a quiet voice, which was meant to sound spooky.

'Has anyone seen all seven?' one of the women in the crowd wanted to know.

'Who believes in ghosts?' Gina whispered to her little group.

'You know I don't,' said Lorelei, ever the pragmatist.

'Um . . . I don't think so,' Paula said when Gina looked at her.

'I'm not sure . . .' Maddison answered.

'What about you?' Dermot asked Gina.

'No way!' she insisted. 'They're just stories. Stories made up to frighten the kids.'

Dermot looked at her with his eyebrows raised. 'I totally believe in ghosts,' he said – so seriously that Gina immediately suspected he was teasing.

'No way you do!' she exclaimed. 'You don't even believe in Santa Claus.'

'Santa Claus! Of course I believe in Santa Claus, and I believe in ghosties . . .' He gave a deep, mock horror-film laugh as the guide motioned for them all to follow him into the house.

'We're going down to the vault,' Dermot explained. 'You won't believe how big it is – with lots of little passages leading off in different directions.'

Down in the darkness of the cellar, the tourists instinctively huddled close together in the damp chill.

'Edinburgh vaults had all kinds of uses,' the guide was telling them. 'The poor used to live in them; plague victims were often kept underground, so they couldn't infect anyone else. Until very recently, every vault came with its own family of rats.'

Gina shuddered. Of course there weren't rats down

here now, she tried to tell herself. But in the flickering darkness, lit only by the two torches in the guide's hands, things which might have been funny upstairs or out on the street were a bit more creepy.

'Look around – feel free to wander about,' the guide added. 'I'll light a few tapers and you can go off in groups. See if you find anything interesting . . . or unusual.'

As soon as Dermot had a taper in his hand, he slipped his arm through Gina's and whispered against her hair, 'Shall we try and sneak off?'

These words made Gina giggle and tingle. When Dermot took her hand in his, there was a momentary fizz of static.

As the crowd of tourists spread out, Dermot hurried her towards a little side passage. As soon as they had rounded the corner, they paused, looking into each other's eyes, totally caught up in what they knew was going to happen next.

Their heads moved together, and although it had only been twenty-four hours since they'd last kissed like this, it felt too long. Much, much too long.

Gina leaned back against the damp brick wall. She slid her hands in under Dermot's coat collar and scarf so she could touch the soft skin of his neck.

She felt his teeth bump against hers and opened her

mouth a little further. Opening her eyes slightly, she saw Dermot's cheek in fascinating close-up in the dim light of the taper. Just beyond his shoulder, holding a taper of her own, she also saw her mother.

'Er . . . erm . . .' Lorelei cleared her throat, before adding frostily, 'Excuse me!'

Chapter Six

As soon as Finn had chosen his seat at the dinner table, Amy picked the chair opposite. This way, she thought to herself, she'd have something good to look at in the gloomy dining room, and something entertaining to take her mind off the meal. She'd had dinner at Blacklough Hall often enough to know that the supply of snacks hidden in her luggage was essential. Cooking and eating just weren't N-B priorities.

It was easy to understand why Mr and Mrs N-B were so slim; what was not so easy to understand was how their children had grown so tall. Maybe that was due to boarding-school food: Niffy always ate enormous portions at school.

'So tell us all about St Jude's,' Finn said, shooting Amy a grin. 'What's happening? What's the latest? How is your Californian friend settling in?'

'Oh, she's fine,' Niffy said, before slurping up a

mouthful of the bitter spinach soup. 'She's written a play or something, hasn't she?'

Niffy wasn't totally up-to-date with the school gossip because she'd insisted that she wasn't going back to St J's until she knew that her mum was on the road to recovery.

'Yeah, there's this house competition: four plays written by pupils are going to be performed, and Gina's is one of them,' Amy explained. 'I'm going to audition for the main part because she thinks it would suit me,' she added, because it suddenly seemed important that Finn should know about this.

'I had a friend who was in all the plays at school and now she's a famous actress,' Mrs N-B chipped in.

'Really?' Amy asked, astonished. The idea of Mrs N-B being friends with anyone famous or even slightly glamorous was strange. She was the kind of woman who wore the same dresses for twenty-odd years and spent a lot of time weeding.

'Yes, Gwen Smith-Turner,' she said. 'Maybe you've heard of her?'

Now Amy was open-mouthed with astonishment. 'You know her?'

Gwen Smith-Turner was one of the poshest, most glamorous, most utterly famous actresses in the country.

'Oh yes, very well,' Mrs N-B confirmed.

'She was at St Jude's?' Amy gasped.

'Mmmm. I've got some photos. I'll look them out for you later.'

Amy would have liked to ask about a hundred more questions, but then Finn said, 'Aha, so you're a fellow thespian?' His arching eyebrows threatened to rise up into his hair.

'Huh?'

'He just means he's into theatre stuff as well,' Niffy explained through a mouthful of bread.

'Do you like acting too?' Amy asked, aware that she was finding it hard to take her eyes off Finn. And also aware that whenever she looked at him, he was already looking at her, which made her fizz with some kind of nervous energy.

'No, I like to direct,' Finn replied. 'I'm hoping I'll get the chance to direct the school play next term. In the meantime I've got a nice little video camera – I like to make films. I've got a couple of long-suffering friends who don't mind doing a bit of acting for me . . .'

There was a pause and Finn carried on looking at Amy as Amy carried on looking at Finn.

She wondered if he was thinking what she was thinking: would he like to film her acting for his video camera? That would be so intimate and intriguing . . . The thought of it was making her shiver.

Amy was enjoying her secret little crush so much. It seemed to be growing stronger by the second, even though it was only yesterday that she'd told her last crush to get lost.

The previous object of Amy's affections had been Jason: so handsome and so fantastic when he was right there in front of you, but completely unreliable, thoughtless – and even a cheat. Yes, her last crush had left her crushed.

But Jason was sooo yesterday. Today, right here, right now, was all about Finn.

Just how nice and how interested did Finn seem? He was Niffy's brother, and Niffy was her best friend in the whole world – there was no one more in tune with Amy than Niffy – so didn't it make sense that Finn and Amy would be a perfect match?

'What are the plans for tomorrow?' Mr N-B asked, forcing Finn and Amy to tear their gazes from each other.

'Well, Amy will borrow wellies and anoraks and stuff,' Niffy began, 'and then we'll tramp about giving the dogs their run in the morning and maybe she'll watch me do a bit of riding, then we'll head into the village for lunch. How does that sound?'

'Yeah . . .' Amy agreed dubiously. On the journey

down, the prospect of borrowing Niffy's old wellies and wax jackets had seemed bad enough, but now that Finn was around to see her – it was horrible.

'I thought you didn't like horses?' Finn asked.

Amy gave what she hoped was a tactful shrug-smile. She didn't want to hurt Niffy's feelings – but on the other hand, maybe Finn was going to suggest something else she could be doing with him while Niffy was riding.

'Well, when you're riding, Niff, I could show Amy some of my films – I mean, if you're interested, Amy; if that's the kind of thing you—'

Amy felt her heart leap with excitement.

'Oh, for goodness' sake, Finn!' Mr N-B cut in. 'I'm sure Amy doesn't want to spend hours trying to make sense of your arty twaddle.' He turned to Amy. 'I think Finn's been over-exposed to experimental Russian films at school. Biggest load of gloomy nonsense I've ever seen.'

'Well, Dad, you are someone who thinks Monty Python is the epitome of cinematic achievement,' Finn said crossly.

'Monty Python – absolutely hilarious,' Mr N-B insisted, laughing at the mere thought.

Before Amy could insist that arty twaddle was the one thing she would most like to spend tomorrow morning watching, Mrs N-B offered her suggestion.

'Amy, when Niffy is riding, why don't you spend some time with me? We'll look out those old school photos of Gwen and maybe do a bit of baking. I've heard that you make an unbelievably good Glasgow scone.'

'The Dough School recipe,' Amy confirmed. 'My gran taught it to me.'

'Great idea!' Finn was looking at Amy again. 'I love scones – almost as much as I love doughnuts.'

'Mmm,' Niffy and Finn said together. '*Doughnuts.*'

They were doing Homer Simpson. It was a brother-sister thing, Amy realized with a tiny pang of jealousy.

'Can I watch you make the scones?' Finn asked.

But just as Amy imagined an hour or two in the cosy kitchen laughing at Finn's jokes, smiling into Finn's eyes and making Finn fall down in amazement at her incredible scones, Mrs N-B dashed her hopes.

'Don't be silly! I want Amy to myself, Finn – and anyway, you are the clumsiest person I know. No, you definitely can't help us make scones!'

Was it just Amy's imagination or did a look of disappointment flicker across Finn's face?

Chapter Seven

Gina couldn't help giggling when she read the text Dermot had just sent her: IS YR MOM STILL NOT TALKING 2 U?

SHE'S FORGIVEN ME BUT NOT U, she texted back.

O 2 BAD, came the reply.

HV TO STOP TXTING COS MAKING ME C-SICK, she told him.

Because she, Paula, Maddison and Lorelei were now on a ferry. This was part two of her mother's frantic week of sightseeing.

As soon as Edinburgh had been 'done', Lorelei had hired a car and loaded up the three girls and all their luggage: they were off to the tiny little island in the Inner Hebrides where Lorelei had spent so many summer holidays when she was a girl.

'I can't wait to show you Colonsay,' she kept telling them. 'It's this beautiful, amazing place. I bet it's hardly changed at all since I used to holiday there. Twenty . . .

oh my goodness, over *thirty* years ago now . . .' She'd seemed slightly shocked by the calculation.

Gina, Paula and Maddison were all excited by the trip. On the map, the island of Colonsay was a tiny speck of land miles and miles out to sea. Coming from a country where everything was on a vast scale, the Californians loved the idea of visiting somewhere so small.

Once they were up on the ferry deck, watching the mainland slip away, Gina's mother came over and caught her texting. 'Dermot?' she asked.

Gina quickly folded her phone away.

After the snog, relations between Lorelei and Dermot had been frosty for the rest of the ghost tour, despite his best efforts to jolly things along.

'Stop making jokes!' Gina had hissed at him. 'You're just making things worse.'

All thoughts of Dermot being invited back to the hotel for a cosy evening in the lounge were dispelled as soon as the ghost tour was over: Lorelei had said firmly, 'Nice to meet you, Dermot. I hope you don't have so much trouble getting your bus home.' She'd shaken his hand, shot him a pained smile, then put her arm in Gina's and frog-marched her daughter along the pavement before she could even so much as say goodbye.

'Mom!' Gina had complained. 'That wasn't very nice.'

Now, Lorelei pushed her sunglasses up onto her head and reached over to move several loose strands of hair out of Gina's face. 'I didn't give Dermot much of a chance, did I?' she asked her daughter.

'No,' Gina agreed.

'I'm sorry.'

This wasn't a word Gina heard her mother say often, so she felt a little surprised.

'It's just . . . you're so far away from home over here,' Lorelei began. 'I want you to be safe and loved and looked after. I don't want you to be hurt or heart-broken, or for anything bad to happen to you ever. Can you understand that?'

'Yeah, sure,' Gina said, her voice gentle. 'But nothing about Dermot has been bad. He's been really kind to me, and he and the dorm girls are the people who've made me feel most welcome here. They're my friends.'

'He just seemed such a . . . joker,' Lorelei said. 'Not at all serious. Cheeky even.'

Gina sighed. 'I knew you'd think that. I kept telling him not to joke with you. He's really smart, Mom. He's trying to get into Edinburgh University next year, and he's the kind of guy who does dates at art galleries. Really,' she added, almost shyly, 'he's cool. I like him a lot.'

'Yeah, well, I could see that from the way you were kissing him. That was just a little too hot for my liking,' her mom told her.

'We were just kissing,' Gina said firmly.

'Keep it cool – I don't want you to get hurt.'

'I'll be fine. I promise,' Gina replied.

The ferry was heading out into the open sea, and the waves were beginning to rock the deck up and down.

'This is really exciting.' Gina smiled at her mother. 'Did you come to this island every year?'

'Yeah, summer holidays and Easter. All four of us, playing on the beaches for weeks and weeks on end . . . Well, that's what it felt like – but you know, Dad was so busy, the breaks were probably only a fortnight long.'

'So busy, huh?' Gina repeated to herself as Lorelei's phone bleeped like a needy electronic baby in her handbag and took her attention away once again.

Twenty minutes later, the waves were beginning to grow larger and Gina heard Maddison give a moan.

'It's getting worse,' she said. 'I don't feel so good!'

'How long is this journey?' Paula asked, looking anxiously out at the choppy water ahead.

'Two hours,' Lorelei told them.

'You've got to be kidding!' Both girls were dismayed.

'Maybe we should go inside, sit down and have some tea,' Lorelei suggested.

'Yeah,' Paula agreed immediately. 'The sea spray is messing with my hair big time.' She put both hands up to her wild, crinkled mane and scrunched it between her fingers.

A cup of tea and a seat didn't help Maddison. As the ferry rolled up and down, she began to look more and more pale and green. Soon she was rushing off to the toilets to be sick. Afterwards she lay limply across three seats and groaned, her eyes shut.

'It might help to go back out on deck,' Lorelei said. 'You're supposed to look at the horizon, I think. That used to help my brother.'

But Maddison just shook her head. She didn't want to move, she didn't want to look; she just wanted this terrible journey to end. In just three days' time they'd be coming back! The thought of this made her groan again.

'Poor you.' Gina stroked Maddison's hair.

'When are we going to get there?' she whimpered.

A quick glance at her watch told Gina there was still over an hour to go, but she wasn't sure if Maddison could stand this news, so instead she just said,

'Shhhhh. Try and have a little nap, then it will pass more quickly.'

It was early afternoon, the sky a steely grey, threatening rain, when the dark green island finally came into view.

There was a small harbour with a couple of buildings beside it, plus the odd cottage and a thin grey ribbon of road leading in twists and turns away from the jetty.

Gina was thinking about the hotel. She'd seen the brochure pictures of the charming rooms with their comfortable beds, the old-fashioned bar and the dining room with its sea view.

They were going to be very well looked after during their visit to the island – her mother had made sure of that. In fact, it was only after Lorelei had found out there was a new hotel there that she'd decided to make the return journey. Her family had always rented an old farmhouse, which she described as 'basic'.

Finally, with bumps, scrapes and a churn of propellers in the water, the ferry docked and the party of Americans climbed back into their car and prepared to drive off to the hotel.

No one wanted to say how bleak and grey the island looked, but they were all thinking it.

'You won't believe how pretty it is as soon as the

cloud breaks,' Lorelei said, as cheerfully as she could, when the car hit land and began to follow the few other vehicles onto the ribbon of road. 'And it gets lots of sunshine,' she added – which, looking at the lead-coloured sky, the girls found hard to believe.

After a ten-minute drive they were pulling up in front of a hotel that looked just as fresh, modern and glamorous as in the brochure.

The mood in the car lifted, and soon everyone was hurrying out with their bags. Gina was thinking about a cream tea; Paula was imagining seafood; Maddison was just desperate to lie down between cool white sheets.

Laden with luggage, they walked through the open front door and into the reception.

'Oh, this was such a good idea,' Lorelei exclaimed. 'I think we're going to have a wonderful time here.'

A blonde woman dressed in a plaid skirt and matching waistcoat appeared behind the desk. She looked concerned.

'Hello . . .' she said tentatively. 'I wasn't expecting anyone off the boat today.'

'Oh, yes, yes,' Lorelei assured her. 'We have two double rooms booked for three nights. From today. Under the name Winkelmann.'

'That can't be right,' the woman told her, looking

very anxious now. 'We had a wedding at the weekend and we're fully booked till Friday.'

The news made the Americans reel.

'No!' Lorelei insisted. 'I have the booking details in my purse. There's been a mistake – you can't possibly be full.'

The woman looked upset, realizing what a terrible situation this was. The hotel was the only one on the island, the ferry had almost certainly left by now, and these people were going to be stranded.

If there had just been two of them, she thought, she might have been able to sleep on a sofa and give up her own room. But four . . . She couldn't accommodate four guests anywhere in her hotel.

'You're not the Californians, are you?' she asked, sounding puzzled. 'I remember taking the booking . . . by email. I have you down for March.'

She began to tap at her computer, determined to show them the reservation and the email which had confirmed it.

March?

Then, all at once, Lorelei understood her new PA's mistake. In Britain 11/3 means 11 March. In the States, it means 3 November.

'Oh, good grief,' she whispered as she read the confirmation email her PA had sent.

'What are we going to do?' Maddison cried, just as everyone realized how serious this was. They were stranded on a tiny island, a two-hour boat trip from the mainland, and there was no room at the inn.

'I can't believe this!' Lorelei exclaimed. 'I would have called you myself to double-check the reservation before I left home, but I guess I ran out of time and I just assumed everything would be fine. Oh my goodness!' she said with exasperation. 'Is there a boat later today?'

The woman behind the counter replied as gently as she could, 'Well, no, dear . . . the next boat doesn't come till Thursday.'

'*What?*' Paula, Gina and Maddison exclaimed together, astonished.

'Please don't worry,' the woman reassured them. 'This is an island. We're used to pulling together and sorting things out for ourselves. I really can't fit any of you in here at the hotel, but why don't you go to the lounge, have a seat and a wee cup of coffee, while I make some phone calls. I'm sure we'll be able to sort something out.'

'I thought this was the only hotel?' Gina said.

'Well, yes, but there are other places for tourists to stay. I'm June, by the way,' she told them, then pointed them in the direction of the hotel lounge.

* * *

They were settled on a pair of sofas with two coffees, a cup of tea and a glass of wine on the table in front of them, when June came in with a smile on her face.

'I've found you somewhere,' she announced cheerfully. 'It's not quite as nice as here, but you'll have two double beds and there's a fireplace, so you'll be able to enjoy a cosy blaze at night.'

The Californians looked at her blankly. A fireplace? A cosy blaze? None of them had the slightest idea how to light a fire.

'Come over to us for dinner and breakfast – even lunch if you like. We'll be able to provide that for you without any problem,' June went on. 'Just use the cottage as somewhere to lay your heads at night.'

'Where is it?' Lorelei wondered.

'Not far. I've printed out a map.'

It was only ten minutes away, Lorelei driving slowly along the narrow, unfamiliar road through the damp darkness.

'Is this it? It looks . . . basic,' Maddison asked, looking out of the car window and voicing everyone else's thoughts.

They had pulled up in front of a tiny, dark cottage, surrounded by bare hillside and black rock. Not a tree or even a bush could be seen anywhere.

'The key's under the doormat, apparently. We just go in . . .' Lorelei didn't sound her usual certain self. Maybe her first impression of this gloomy place had thrown her off her stride too.

Lifting up the doormat, she found mud, some scuttling insects and a key with a large paper label tied round it which read FRONT DOOR.

She fitted it into the lock and pushed open the small, pale blue door. It was stiff and she had to put all her weight behind it as it scraped over the stone floor. She groped about for a light switch and finally found one. When she threw it, the dim hum of an energy-saving light bulb started up. As the girls followed Lorelei into the cottage, in the pale orangey glow they could see a tiny sitting room with three small chairs and a blackened fireplace.

Compared to the luxury and glamour of the hotel, this was basic.

'Oh Jeez!' Maddison couldn't help exclaiming. 'Is this it?'

'What are we going to do here all night?' Paula asked.

'Huddle round the light bulb for warmth,' Maddison suggested.

'Well, maybe it won't be so bad once we figure out how to set fire to those logs over there,' Gina said, trying to get everyone to be more upbeat

But the others weren't happy at all. The two bedrooms were only just big enough for the small double bed each one contained.

'We're going to be a bit too cosy,' Paula said to Maddison when they saw their bed.

'I don't think so.' Maddison blew out to demonstrate the cloud of steam her breath made in the chilly room. 'Omigod! I haven't seen that since I went skiing in Aspen.'

All these complaints were winding Gina up. Her friends were finding something to criticize everywhere they looked.

'I can't sleep in this cold,' Paula whined.

'There's an electric heater over there,' Gina said, pointing to the corner of the bedroom. 'We'll get it plugged in. I bet there's one in our room too, Mom – and c'mon, surely between the four of us, we can get a fire started?'

By six o'clock, however, it had become clear that there was an art to making fires.

Gina had enthusiastically set fire to all the newspaper twists and all the strips of kindling, but still the logs remained stubbornly un-lit.

'This isn't going to work!' Maddison moaned.

'Why don't we just go to bed? It's dark enough out there,' Paula grumbled.

Gina really wanted this holiday to work: for her, for her friends and for her mother. Her mother never took vacations – if this was a disaster, maybe she'd never take another! Gina didn't want to hear anyone else complaining about another thing.

'No!' she insisted. 'We're not going to moan and we're not going to sulk. We're going to go back to the hotel for a lovely dinner and, Mom, they might have wi-fi for you to download all your urgent emails – and hey, maybe June can teach us how to light a fire.'

Chapter Eight

The monumental plate of scones that Amy had made with Mrs N-B was demolished by Finn and Niffy.

'I think this is what you call a bun fight!' Amy had joked as she'd watched brother and sister argue fiercely about who was going to get the last scone.

'Manners maketh man,' Mr N-B announced from his end of the table as Niffy struck Finn on the back of the knuckles with her knife and declared, 'Hands off!'

'Children! Behave! I can make more – Amy's given me the recipe!' Mrs N-B told them.

Once the scones were finished, Mr N-B offered them a lift to the village.

'Yeah!' Finn enthused. 'Niffy and I will take Amy round the sights and then we'll pay a visit to the new tea rooms – because you never know, we might be hungry again by then.'

'Do you want to come?' Niffy turned to her brother

in surprise. 'I thought this was going to be just me and Amy.'

'Please let me come,' Finn said with a mock-pleading expression on his face. 'I'll be very good. If I'm annoying in any way, just kick me.'

'With pleasure,' Niffy assured him.

As they got ready to go, Amy put on her high-heeled red boots and her silky new parka. Niffy shot her a raised eyebrow.

'Aim, it is absolutely peeing out there. You're going to get soaked through. Here . . .' She handed Amy some revolting old waxy Barbour jacket and a pair of wellies crusted with mud and smelling unmistakably of cheese.

'Are these your old ones?' Amy asked.

'Yup.'

'I can't, I just can't,' Amy told her, wrinkling up her nose.

But Niffy insisted, and so Amy found herself sitting next to Finn in the back of the Range Rover in a crackling waxy jacket, last in fashion in the 1980s, and a pair of wellies she was sure Finn could smell.

After a wet and soggy tramp around the village, the three of them went into the tea rooms, where Finn ordered a round of coffees and *ten* doughnuts.

Amy, shocked, had to ask, 'Didn't you eat enough scones?'

'Well, yeah, but you have to try their doughnuts – it would be a crime not to.'

As they sat down, Amy manoeuvred herself into the seat next to Finn's and immediately peeled off her wax jacket, rolled it into a ball and bundled it under the table.

'Sorry – Niffy made me wear it,' she explained. 'And I don't want to talk about the wellies on my feet. In fact I don't even want to *think* about the wellies. She made me,' Amy repeated.

Niffy was up at the counter, collecting the coffees, so there wasn't any real need for Finn to lean close to whisper in her ear, 'We'll get her back . . . I'm plotting a nice little trick for later.'

The touch of his breath against her ear made Amy giddy with nervous excitement. He was great! He really was great. He was so good-looking and so funny and so nice and so friendly, and he was right here, beside her, most definitely interested.

Although she was slightly surprised by how quickly she seemed to have got over Jason, it was a good thing, surely? Wasn't it?

'We have to play tricks – it's all there is to do for fun round here,' Finn went on. 'We can't go and hang out with Angus because he's on a French exchange for the next six weeks or something . . . which is why Niff's so grumpy,' he added, his voice low and confidential again.

Angus was Finn's friend and Niffy's current Boy of Interest. His aunt and uncle happened to live close to Blacklough, so Angus had been spending a lot of time with them recently in order to see more of Niffy.

As Amy's eyes met Finn's, she found herself studying them, trying to make out their colour. They were too dark to be blue, but they weren't quite brown. She stared and saw a mossy, hazel brown with slashes of green radiating out from the iris.

'So . . . what do you think?' Finn asked, and Amy realized with a start that she hadn't listened to a word he'd been saying. She'd been caught a little too helplessly in those fascinating eyes.

'Hmm . . .' she answered, trying not to sound as if she agreed or disagreed. What had he just asked her?

'OK!' He flashed a grin. 'We'll do that later. Here she comes – stop looking so guilty!' he whispered.

Do *what* later?! Amy wondered, feeling alarmed. Was this about the trick? What exactly had she just agreed to?

Niffy brought over the coffees and put a plate loaded with four doughnuts in front of her place. She gulped a great mouthful of coffee down, then headed back to the counter to collect Amy and Finn's doughnuts.

'This is just for now,' Finn said, hurriedly shaking salt over Niffy's plate.

'No!' Amy gasped. 'You can't do that.'

'Can,' Finn replied, plastering a perfectly innocent expression onto his face as Niffy returned with more doughnuts.

'Four each for us and two for you,' Niffy explained.

'You won't be skinny for ever,' Amy commented, as Finn crammed an entire doughnut into his mouth.

'Yeah we will,' Niffy assured her. 'You've seen our mum and dad. Whereas you, Aim, need to get back on that hockey pitch with me or you'll get all squidgy.'

'Huh?' was Amy's embarrassed response. But there was a little sting of truth in the comment. Niffy hadn't been at school for half a term, and without Niffy to inspire her, Amy's interest in hockey had waned and her thighs and waistline had undoubtedly spread. Not by much – but obviously enough for Niffy to notice.

Finn was gulping down his coffee, studiously pretending he hadn't heard any of this, but Amy's cheeks burned because she knew perfectly well that he had.

Suddenly her appetite for doughnuts disappeared completely and she pushed her plate away.

'I wonder how Min's surviving at her auntie's?' Amy said, desperate to change the subject.

'Min will be fine – she's probably taken a physics text-book or two to help the time pass. You know what?' Niffy asked, picking up the first of her sabotaged doughnuts and holding it just in front of her mouth.

Amy flinched. She wanted to say something, she really did.

Niffy bit down. 'I think we'll do the pool tomorrow – get you started with a fifty-lap race and a new fitness regime,' she said through her mouthful.

'The pool? I dunno . . .' Amy hesitated, not wanting to do anything that took her away from Finn. She was trying not to stare at Niffy as she chewed.

Finn had shaken a lot of salt onto that plate, but Niffy ate her way cheerfully through the entire doughnut, and the three others, without uttering a single murmur of complaint.

Only when her plate was scraped clean did she say, 'Must have burned my tongue on the coffee – those tasted odd.'

When both Finn and Amy burst out laughing, Niffy stared at them in confusion. 'Have I missed the joke?' she asked.

'Never mind,' Finn said.

'No, it's nothing,' Amy insisted. Then Finn gave her a wink, and once again she found herself wondering uncomfortably what exactly she had agreed to do with him later.

Chapter Nine

'What do you think your mom is doing?' Maddison asked as she peered out of the small cottage window into the darkness. 'It looks like she's trying to climb up that hill.'

'Is she holding her BlackBerry?' Gina asked.

'Umm . . . there's a light in her hand. Is that her phone?'

'Definitely. Just what I thought. My mom is out there in the darkness, in the rain, climbing a hill, trying to get a signal so she can download her email, then phone up her PA and yell at her for messing up our holiday,' Gina informed them.

'Jeez . . .' Paula flopped down onto one of the chairs and stared into the empty fireplace.

'Anyone want to take June's fire-starting advice?' Gina asked.

Paula shook her head. 'Isn't it kinda late?'

Maddison was looking at the tiny bookcase. 'Two

fish cookbooks, one old thriller and a Monopoly set. They sure know how to have a good time up here,' she grumbled.

'Is there a TV?' Paula asked.

'No,' Maddison answered immediately.

At least dinner had been good. They had spent three whole hours in the cosy hotel, eating, drinking and chatting. But the wi-fi connection had been down, and June had assured Lorelei that there wasn't any hope of getting a signal – apparently only one network covered the island, and it wasn't hers.

While they sat in the dining room, Gina couldn't help noticing that her mom was finding it hard to relax. Her eyes kept straying to her phone as if she could somehow will it into life.

But their delicious dinner in the lovely hotel had the unfortunate effect of making the cottage seem all the more gloomy and unwelcoming.

'My mom doesn't really do vacations,' Gina told her friends now. 'She and Mick go on business trips and take the odd weekend break – but that's about it. We don't do family trips. Mom doesn't like to be away from work for long. So I really want her to have a good time here.'

When neither of her friends made any reply to this, Gina went on, 'I'm really sorry we're not at the hotel, but I don't think this place is so bad. It just needs to warm up – we'll get used to it.'

'I thought it would be cool to be on an island, but it feels like we've gone back in time,' Paula whinged.

'Yeah. The land that time forgot,' Maddison added. 'I mean, we are so far away from anything and it is so boring out here. What are we going to do tomorrow? Go for walks in the rain?'

'Just think about it, Gina – your mom used to be stuck here for weeks on end. No wonder she lives in California and never takes a vacation any more. She's traumatized!'

'I don't think you're being very nice,' Gina snapped, annoyed with both of them now. 'The cottage isn't that bad, and I'm looking forward to seeing round the island.'

'Not that bad? Have you even been in the bathroom?!' Maddison protested.

'Yeah, maybe you've got used to this kind of thing at your boarding school – but we still have standards,' Paula said.

'Standards!' Gina spluttered.

'Yeah, we like something a little more twenty-first century, or even twentieth century,' Maddison added.

'You mean you're both totally spoiled and pampered princesses who can't survive one night without a Jacuzzi and a pump-action shower. Babies!' Gina declared. 'Or should that be *Bar*bies?!'

Oh! That sounded much angrier than she'd intended. But she was so annoyed with them. They'd all been looking forward to this trip for so long, and now it just seemed to be going horribly wrong.

'I'm going to bed,' Maddison said, standing up and crossing her arms huffily.

'Me too.' Paula joined her, so now both friends were standing there glaring at her.

'Fine!' Gina said.

They carried on looking at her; maybe they thought she should apologize.

'I'm not going to say sorry,' Gina blurted out. 'You're being babies. The girls in my dorm wouldn't be sitting around complaining about not being in a five-star hotel. They would have lit the fire, opened up the Monopoly and tried to see the funny side!'

'Oh, really!' Paula exclaimed. 'Well, maybe your new friends should have come on your island trip with you instead of us.'

'Maybe!' Gina replied. 'All you've done is whine ever

since we got here: *Oooh it's so cold, oooh it's so dark, oooh my hair, oooh my shoes, oooh why can't we be in the luxury hotel with satellite TV and wi-fi?* It's supposed to be travel. An adventure!' she told them. 'You two are about as adventurous as a couple of old ladies!'

Now Gina had done it.

Now both Paula and Maddison were properly angry with her.

'Scotland stinks, Gina. Get used to it!' Paula retorted. 'Like Maddison said, it's like travelling back in time. To the dark ages! I wish we'd never bothered to come.'

'We gave up a really good Halloween party for this trip!' Maddison added.

'And I'm kind of wondering why! Do you even want us here?' Paula asked.

'Yeah, it's pretty obvious we're your second-best friends now anyway,' Maddison threw in. 'I don't know why you asked us over.'

Gina sat bolt upright and might have said a whole load of other things she would later regret, but then they all heard Lorelei stepping onto the front porch.

'C'mon, Maddison, there's nothing to do here,' Paula snapped.

And with that, the pair stalked off into the tiny bedroom they were sharing.

Gina could feel her cheeks burning with anger and embarrassment, but she didn't say anything to stop her friends leaving the room. Right now, she meant every single word she'd said. Right now, she just felt so angry and upset and disappointed that she couldn't possibly have thought of anything nice to say to them.

She had been looking forward to this holiday too. She'd had all sorts of lovely pictures in her mind of what they would do on the island: of them all exploring together – maybe hiring a boat; of her mom taking her to all the places she used to visit as a child. She'd thought it would be so much fun. But it was all going wrong.

Before Lorelei could even make it in through the door, Gina left the sitting room and went into the bedroom she was sharing with her mom. Sitting on the edge of the bed, she felt tears well up in the back of her throat, but she struggled to choke them back down.

The front door scraped open and Lorelei called out, 'Hellooo, where is everyone?'

Then her face appeared at the bedroom door. 'It's a bit early for bed, isn't it?' she asked.

'Is it?' Gina huffed. 'There's nothing else to do here,

is there? Paula and Maddison have gone to bed and you don't want to talk to me,' she accused her mother. 'You're too busy trying to talk to someone in your office on the other side of the world!'

Chapter Ten

'Shhhh! I think I can hear something . . .'

Amy, crouching down, knee-deep in straw, thought this had to be the most ridiculous thing she'd ever done. She was only here because of Finn. This was his big idea, his clever trick, and although she didn't entirely approve of it, she couldn't think of anything she'd rather be doing right now than crouching, knee-deep in straw, beside him.

Whenever Finn's elbow brushed against hers, even through the layers of jumpers and jackets, she felt a thrill. More than anything else, she wanted his face, which she was studying so carefully in profile, to turn towards her, smile and – her stomach clenched at the thought – lean down towards hers. Amy knew for certain that she wanted Finn to kiss her, and somehow, before half term was over, she was sure it was going to happen. She'd make sure it happened.

Even if she had to spend the rest of her time here

crouching down in straw in the darkness at the back of Ginger's stable.

'This will be OK?' Amy had asked anxiously as Finn had opened the stable door and given Ginger a friendly pat.

'Fine,' Finn had assured her. 'Ginger's more like the family pet than a horse. We've had him since he was a foal ... Good boy.' He walked casually past the huge animal, Amy following nervously behind him.

Once Finn and Amy were at the back of the stable, Ginger seemed to forget all about them and went on tugging hay out of his net with great grinding teeth.

As soon as Amy was crouched down beside Finn, she thought Ginger's behind looked very big and very strong.

'Couldn't he just kick us – without even meaning to?' she asked Finn.

'Nah, he wouldn't,' Finn promised her. 'This is going to be hilarious,' he added. 'Shhhhh! I think I can hear something ...'

Amy hunkered down in the darkness, strained her ears and waited.

Now, sure enough, she could hear footsteps. Niffy hadn't taken long to get here. As soon as she'd left the dining room with the words, 'I'm going to change into my old clothes and settle Ginger down for the night,' Finn and Amy had jumped into action.

Without giving Mr and Mrs N-B much explanation, they'd fled out of the dining room too, grabbed jackets and wellies and raced down to the stable to get here ahead of Niffy.

'Hello, my darling, how are you doing?' Niffy's voice drifted across to them. 'Have you had a lovely supper . . . have you? Where's my clever, handsome boy then . . .'

Niffy approached her beloved horse. She stroked his head, then pulled him in close and nuzzled her head into his neck.

'Hello, my lovely boy,' she said, the words a little muffled against his coat. 'Who's my good boy, then? Is it you?'

Then to Amy's surprise, Finn uttered a surprisingly convincing 'Naaaaaaahay,' in reply to Niffy's question.

'Yes, you are – yes, you're my darling . . .' Niffy said, her head still buried in the horse's neck, delighted to have got a response from him.

Amy looked at Finn and saw that his face was tight with suppressed laughter. Now she wanted to laugh too. She had no idea where this was going, but she had a suspicion that however it ended, Niffy was going to be absolutely furious with them for spying on her like this.

'I love you, Ginger,' Niffy went on, her deep affection for her horse spilling out, 'and you love me too, don't you?'

The horse had his nose against Niffy's ear and seemed to be snorting into it.

'Yeeeeeeeeeah,' Finn risked, sounding more boy than horse this time.

For a moment Niffy seemed to freeze.

The horse's nose stayed at her ear and she didn't move at all – perhaps wondering for a split second what on earth she'd heard.

Then she raised her head and looked around. 'Finn?' she asked sharply. 'Finn? Are you in here?'

At this, Finn couldn't contain himself any longer. He exploded in a loud volley of laughter.

Both Niffy and Ginger started and looked in surprise towards the back of the stable.

Amy stood up, anxious to get out as quickly as possible. She'd had quite enough of the smelly straw and the big horse bottom.

'Sorry ... we shouldn't have done that ...' she began, seeing that her friend was absolutely furious.

'Amy?!' Niffy managed to blurt out, feeling a surge of anger, hurt and betrayal flooding through her.

They'd been listening! They'd been spying on her and Ginger ... She would never have spoken to her horse if she'd known they were listening. What she said to Ginger was totally, totally private. This was just so unbelievably rude!

Finn would never have done this without Amy to show off to . . . Amy would never have thought of this without Finn! What was going on with those two?

Then the horrible realization dawned: Amy and Finn were trying to impress each other, and Niffy was their piggy in the middle.

Without another word, she turned on her heel and ran out of the stable.

Chapter Eleven

'Auntie, do you ever use your computer?' Min was faced with the prospect of another day without any word from Greg, the boy she was ever so slightly interested in . . . Well, that was all she was admitting to her friends anyway.

For some reason best known to Min and Greg's parents, neither of them had a mobile phone, so their friendship relied completely on the Internet.

Well, in fact, until the night of the Halloween party, their friendship had been an exclusively cyberspace one. They'd met through an on-line physics club. But now that Min had met Greg in the flesh and found him just as nice and cute-looking in person as he was on-line, she wanted to email him all the time, and the prospect of a half-term without a single sentence from him was unbearable.

'Not much,' Min's auntie replied.

'But you have a dial-up modem?' Min asked,

looking at the hulk of grey computer parked in a messy corner of the room; books and papers were piled on top of its keyboard.

'Huh?' Auntie called over her shoulder from the kitchen.

'The Internet?'

'Oh yes . . . the Internet, yes – but I don't use it much.'

Min could see that. She wondered how slow this old dinosaur could be. Surely if she was patient, she could dial up a connection and then eventually connect to her googlemail account. Then she could email Greg and, even better, download whatever email he might have sent her over the past couple of days. She'd only had one tiny, brief message from him since the party and she was desperate to hear more.

'Can I switch it on?' Min asked her aunt.

'Yes,' she replied, 'but not for long. I don't like it to block up the phone line.' Auntie was still in the kitchen. She was always in the kitchen. No matter how much Min offered to help, the kitchen work was never done, according to her aunt. There was yet another huge meal to cook for her enormous bear of a husband, and yet another huge meal to clean up and clear away. So it went on from breakfast, through mid-morning snack, lunch and afternoon snack, to dinner.

It was very hard to get Auntie out of the house for even half an hour before she had to get back to her cooking schedule.

Eagerly Min cleared the books, papers and other stuff off the keyboard and dusted the computer screen. She was good with computers – no surprise there: she was pretty good at everything, apart from maybe French and certain bits of the biology syllabus. But computers? Easy.

Ducking down under the desk, she plugged in the machine and made sure all the relevant leads, wires and cables were connected. Then she switched it on. It hummed, clanked and bleeped into life.

Several agonizingly slow minutes later, a very simple blue screen with just a few icons was staring back at her. She clicked on the Internet connection, and the whirring and high-pitched bleeping that took her way back to the days before broadband started up.

This was going to take some time, she reminded herself. Maybe she should go and make some tea while the computer came slowly back to life.

Coming back over to the desk with her mug, Min saw the Internet page finally up and ready, and clicked on it to begin. The screen promptly froze and a red-bordered message began to flash up in front of her.

'How long has it been since you had the computer on?' she asked her aunt.

'Oh, I'm not sure . . . maybe Christmas?'

Last Christmas! It was nearly this *Christmas!*

According to the message, 11,598 spyware updates and 8,560 virus scans were waiting.

That would take days. Even if Auntie allowed the phone connection to be used by the computer – and she wouldn't – this computer wouldn't be ready to go until half term was over.

DO YOU ACCEPT? the computer screen was asking her.

NO, she clicked.

If only Min had Greg's real address instead of his 'www' one. Then at least she'd be able to write to him. But in the excitement of meeting him for the first time, she hadn't thought of that. She didn't even have his phone number.

Chapter Twelve

Amy could hear Niffy's tread on the stairs. She was stomping up the steps one by one. Just listening to her footsteps, Amy could tell how furious her friend was.

At least she was coming up to see them. Amy and Finn had been waiting for her to appear in the play-room ever since they'd left the stables. But she'd been avoiding them for over an hour.

Quickly Amy got up from the sofa and went over to the door. As soon as Niffy's head emerged at the top of the stairs, she began her apology.

'I'm so sorry, Niffy. It wasn't my idea . . . I'm not sure why I went along with it. It wasn't a nice thing to do . . .'

There was no response, so Amy stumbled on: 'Finn was just trying to make me laugh, I think. Niff? Please, I really am sorry. I think he's sorry too.'

Worse, much worse than saying anything, Niffy just

glared at her. Glared and carried right on past without stopping, without saying a word.

Stomp, stomp, stomp – she went straight on down the corridor and into her bedroom, slamming the door with a deafening crash to make it quite clear that she didn't want anyone to come in and see her.

Amy went back into the TV room, feeling extremely guilty. 'I think I should try and talk to her,' she told Finn.

'Give her five minutes,' he said, and patted the cushion next to his on the sofa. 'Sit – it's just getting to the really interesting bit.' He nodded his head towards the TV.

Amy sat down next to him, and for a few minutes they both pretended to concentrate on the film, although really their minds were not on the screen at all.

Each was focused entirely on the other. They didn't look at each other, but they listened to and felt and sensed each other, all the time looking fixedly ahead, as if what was on TV right now was the most important thing in the world.

Then, all of a sudden, Finn stretched out an arm and placed it on top of the sofa above Amy's shoulder. The arm was definitely on the sofa; it wasn't on her shoulder – but it was there, very close behind her.

She could feel the warmth of it radiating towards her.

She just let it lie there, without any comment, and continued to stare at the screen. Several long, almost entirely breathless minutes went past.

Amy knew she should go and talk to Niffy. She and Finn had just played a horrible trick on her and they had to apologize properly.

But she just couldn't leave the sofa now . . . The arm was behind her head and she was desperate to know where it was heading next.

Amy hadn't moved away from the arm – Finn took this as a good sign. So now he moved his hand very gently onto her hair. Slowly he stroked from the back of her head, down her neck, until his hand was resting on her shoulder.

The touch of his hand against her neck made Amy shiver with surprise and a tingle of excitement.

Finally she took her eyes off the TV and turned her head slowly to face him – wondering, with a clench of nerves in her stomach, what was going to happen next.

Finn was looking at her very calmly. She gazed back, a smile spreading across her face. They were very focused on each other. A deep, long, intense look was burning between them.

Amy's gaze had dropped down to the lips that were moving towards hers. They were thin but shapely, and a vivid pink. They looked soft, and she wanted so much to know what it was going to be like . . . kissing Finn.

She could feel his breath against her cheek, and she reached forward just a tiny bit more so that their lips were now bumping together. The thump of excitement in her chest threatened to jump right out of her throat.

Finn's kiss was needy and interesting, and the longer it went on, the longer Amy wanted it to go on. As he moved his head back, Amy moved hers towards him, not wanting their lips to break apart . . .

The playroom door was several inches ajar, so when Niffy walked towards it, she couldn't help seeing what was going on inside. Her brother's arm was around Amy's shoulders. He was pulling Amy in towards him – Amy's eyes were closed and she was tilting up her face towards his!

Niffy could feel her breath jump and catch in her chest the way it did before any big event: a hockey match, a show-jumping round. Clearly these two really had impressed each other when they'd played that horrible trick on her in the stable. Never mind making her feel like a total idiot, so long as they'd got what they'd wanted out of it.

Piggy in the middle . . . one big green gooseberry – that was all she was going to be for the rest of half term. Fat chance of Amy coming to the pool with her tomorrow – she'd just want to hang around Finn, listening to his every word, laughing at his jokes, slobbering all over his face.

Niffy could feel her hands shake. She balled them into fists to try to steady them. She couldn't just stand here and watch this; listen to these terrible slurping and sucking noises.

What had got into these two? Didn't they realize how horrible this was for her? Didn't they know that this just wasn't right?

'NO!' she suddenly heard herself shouting out. 'No. No. NO!'

Amy and Finn jumped apart at the sound of her voice and turned in astonishment to face her.

Chapter Thirteen

'Gina? Gina!' Lorelei was sitting up in bed, gently shaking her daughter's shoulder. 'Wake up, baby. You've just got to see the colour of the sky.'

When Gina finally opened her eyes, they focused on the small window set in the white wall and she registered the astonishing deep blue colour. For a moment, hovering between sleeping and waking, she thought she was back home. It was like a Californian sky, but somehow a clearer, cooler blue.

Lorelei got out of bed and went over to the window to take a closer look. 'Wow, we're right beside the sea! We couldn't see it in the dark last night. Look! Look down there.'

Gina got up and went to stand beside her mom. Together they looked at the sandy beach only five hundred metres away; it led down towards a bright turquoise-blue sea.

'Wow!' Gina breathed. 'That is soooo pretty.'

'I think I recognize that beach.' Lorelei sounded excited. 'I think we used to go there. Isn't it beautiful? C'mon on, get dressed. Let's go outside and take a look.'

As she and Gina pulled on jeans, boots and big warm sweaters, Lorelei had an idea. 'OK, we'll get the girls up and we'll all walk down to the hotel for breakfast. The fresh air will wake us up and make us hungry, and anyway, we can't waste one minute of the sunshine – it might be gone in half an hour.'

Now, Gina knew that this really was true: she remembered the Scottish saying: 'If you don't like the weather, come back in five minutes,' because that's how changeable it was up here.

Although she liked the idea of walking to the hotel, she got dressed deliberately slowly: she didn't want to have to wake Paula and Maddison. All the things they'd said to each other last night were coming back to her word for word.

It wasn't exactly the kind of argument that was just going to disappear overnight, was it? A little part of her hoped that it was, because now that the sun was shining and her mom was in a good mood, Gina felt much happier too, and although Paula and Maddison had been really annoying, she regretted everything she could remember saying to them.

But she wasn't ready to say sorry . . . Well, not just yet. Well, not unless maybe they said it first . . . So she stayed in her bedroom, taking an extra-long time to dress and then brush her long golden hair before pulling it into a ponytail. She liked the way she looked this morning: tight, light-blue jeans, clumpy brown biker boots and a chunky caramel-coloured cashmere jumper; just a little slick of pink lip gloss, and then she felt ready to face the day.

Gina could hear Lorelei talking to Maddison and Paula in the sitting room. They were all ready to go; they were just waiting for her to make an appearance.

Taking a deep breath, Gina went into the little sitting room. 'Hi . . .' she said with a little shrug of her shoulders, avoiding eye contact with Paula and Maddison.

'Hi,' they both said back, with about as much enthusiasm as she'd put into the word.

'OK? All set? Got your walking shoes on? And windcheaters, just in case it suddenly pours on us?' Lorelei was asking with a smile – she'd obviously not registered the tension in the air.

She opened the cottage door and let in the most amazing view. The bright, bright blue seemed to go on for as far as the eye could see, turquoise sky meeting turquoise sea in a seamless join way out over the horizon.

'Isn't this fantastic!' Lorelei exclaimed. 'I can't believe how beautiful it is. I remembered it being absolutely wonderful, but I still can't quite believe it. When we arrived yesterday in the gloom and the wet, I thought I'd made a huge mistake. I thought maybe it was only pretty here in the summer. But no, it really is breathtaking all year round.'

'In between storms and rain and darkness,' Gina reminded her.

'C'mon, let's get out there!' Lorelei urged them.

They left the house and began to follow the small winding road down towards the hotel. The wind was chilly and brisk, but the bright golden sunshine lifted Lorelei's spirits further.

'I'm finally relaxing,' she told Gina. 'This feels good.'

Gina couldn't help smiling back at her mom. Even though Paula and Maddison didn't seem ready to cheer up yet, she could still smile at her mom.

'There are some places we have to visit while the weather's like this,' Lorelei went on. 'There's a big sheltered beach I remember, where the seals come right in and lie around and roll in the sand, just like fat brown tourists in Florida . . . seriously!' she added when Paula giggled. 'And a boat! You guys would like to go out in a boat, wouldn't you? While the weather's so beautiful and the sea is calm.'

The three girls stole glances at each other, scowled and shrugged half-heartedly.

'Where's your sense of adventure, girl scouts?' Lorelei teased. 'OK, how about I dare the three of you to go out in a rowing boat? Does that fire you up any more?'

'Sure,' Gina said first.

'Mmm,' Paula and Maddison added with non-committal shrugs.

'What's up with you guys?' Lorelei wanted to know. 'Did no one sleep well?'

This didn't get much of a response, but she told them cheerfully, 'You'll probably all feel much better after a good breakfast.'

Gina wasn't so sure. She was wondering how to get out of being stuck on some stupid boat with two stupid friends who'd flown halfway across the world just to fall out with her.

They made their way along the road, which twisted and turned and eventually took them high above the beach. Gina watched in amazement as her mother took her BlackBerry out of her pocket. Surely she wasn't going to start her search for a signal this early in the day?

'Mom!' Gina warned. 'I thought you were starting to relax.'

'I am,' Lorelei said with a smile, and with that she tossed the phone casually out over the edge.

Open-mouthed with surprise, Gina, Paula and Maddison watched as it spun several times, glinting in the sun, before hitting the water with a little splash.

'Huh?' Gina said, turning to her mom with a grin. 'You're kidding!'

'No,' Lorelei assured her. 'Don't worry, it's insured!'

Chapter Fourteen

Amy sat at the Nairn-Bassett kitchen table and picked at her breakfast anxiously. She was the first one up – apart from Mr and Mrs N-B. Last night, after Niffy had caught her and Finn snogging on the sofa, Amy had tried to speak to her friend.

She'd knocked on her bedroom door, and when there had been no reply, she had tried speaking to her through it, but still no word had come from Niffy.

Obviously the joke with Ginger, followed by the sight of Finn and Amy getting . . . erm . . . cuddly, had been too much for her.

Amy tried to see it from her friend's point of view, but really, what was her problem? Amy was sure that if she had a big brother, she'd love him to go out with Niffy. Wouldn't it be fun? Shouldn't it all be cosy and friendly?

All right, all right, the Ginger prank had been cruel, and Amy could understand her friend getting in a right royal huff about that – but what exactly was wrong with Amy kissing Niffy's big brother? What was wrong with it?

'Nif, I'm really sorry about Ginger,' Amy had said to the door last night. 'I . . . we . . . should never have done that. I'm really sorry . . .' Then she'd paused, racking her brain for something else to say. She wondered if her friend was even listening to her.

'I really like Finn,' Amy had added, feeling a leap of excitement in her stomach as she said the words. 'I'm sorry that you mind . . . Niff?' She had banged on the door once again. 'Let me in. Please.'

But there had been no reply, not even the slightest sound of movement, so after a few minutes Amy had decided to leave her. Maybe she'd have calmed down by the morning.

Plus there had been the lure of going back to the playroom – back to the sofa with Finn.

'Come here,' Finn had ordered with a smile when she'd returned.

Then the sofa had become a small enclosed world where no one and nothing else mattered – except how good it felt to hold Finn's face in her hands and put her mouth against his and explore all the interesting tastes and touches and places that she felt so curious to know about.

The kitchen door creaked open, and there, in a shabby old tartan dressing gown, with her hair all wild and on end, stood Niffy. She looked really groggy. In total contrast to Amy, who was dressed, washed, lightly made up, with her hair beautifully smooth and combed.

'Hi, Niffy,' Amy said brightly.

This just earned her a grunt in response.

'Lou, manners!' Mrs N-B snapped. 'I know you're not worth talking to until you've eaten half a loaf of bread, but at least say hello.'

'Hello, Amy,' Niffy said, but totally stiffly.

'Hi,' Amy said back. 'How are you doing? Did you sleep OK?' She was trying to sound as nice and as cheerful and as friendly as she possibly could, to make it clear that she wanted to be forgiven.

Niffy sat down at the other end of the table from Amy and poured out a mug of tea. 'I met Finn on the stairs – apparently you two are doing some filming together today. How nice.' Her eyes flashed angrily at Amy. 'I'll just go to the pool on my own then. At least that way *I'll* still be able to get into my school skirt.'

The hand bringing the thickly buttered toast laden with marmalade towards Amy's mouth froze in mid-air.

* * *

'And . . . action,' Finn instructed.

Amy turned to face the camera with an exaggerated scowl on her face.

On her head was an old tweed flat cap, borrowed from the Nairn-Bassett cupboard; she was also wearing one of Niffy's frayed and muddy waxed jackets.

'D'you know what I think about television today?' she asked in a deep, posh voice that sounded quite uncannily like Mr Nairn-Bassett's. 'I think it's all utter twaddle. Utter twiddle-twaddle and poppycock.'

Finn was finding it hard to film and refrain from bursting out laughing.

'Now, in my day,' Amy went on, still in the deep, posh voice, 'if you wanted to have a laugh, you went out with some of your rugger chaps and you'd go to some poor old chap and pull down his trousers. *De-bagging*, we called it. Yes, that was what we did for fun.'

Finn was beginning to sweat with the effort of not laughing.

'Then along came that Monty Python lot. They were all right. They understood what fun was all about. It was about telling jokes in a posh voice and walking about looking like a complete twit and all that kind of thing. They were funny. But since then . . . downhill all the way. Complete and utter twaddle.'

Amy had tried to avoid Finn's eye as she was saying all this, but the more the camera shook, the harder this became.

Finally she looked at him directly and the two burst into squawks of helpless laughter. Even if Mr N-B himself had walked in at that moment and told them not to laugh, they wouldn't have been able to stop.

Unfortunately it was Niffy, just back from her trip to the swimming pool, who walked in.

She opened the door of the playroom, saw them both falling about, helpless with hilarity, and assumed at once that they were having some sort of private joke about her, especially as Amy was wearing her jacket.

'Making fun of me again?' she snarled, then turned to leave, and slammed the door behind her.

Chapter Fifteen

Was this really a good idea? Gina couldn't help wondering as she headed towards the cold, wet and completely uninviting sea.

A big, round, bearded guy by the name of Logan had rented them a rowing boat. He'd done it with an unmistakable twinkle in his eye – as if, *yes*, he was agreeing to this, but *no*, he didn't think the girls were up to it.

'So ye can all swim?' he'd asked – *twinkle, twinkle*.

When they had all nodded sulkily, he'd asked, 'But can ye row?'

'Well, kind of . . . I've done it a bit,' Paula had replied.

'It's very calm out there, otherwise I wouldn't let ye. Stay close to the shore, so I can keep an eye on ye, and come back in as soon as the rowers get tired,' he told them. 'Oh, and you'll all have to wear lifejackets, ye know that.'

He'd directed them to a pile of what looked like fat, yellow, smelly cushions.

'These?' Maddison had asked, scrunching up her nose.

Now, the three of them, still in a terrible mood with each other, were marching towards the water, puffed up with the jackets like yellow frogs. Logan was dragging the boat along behind them on a little wheeled trailer.

The sun had gone in behind a blanket of cloud, so the water looked mercilessly steely and cold. Lorelei stood way behind them at the top of the beach, wrapped in a coat, scarf, hat and boots, giving them the odd wave of encouragement.

'We used to spend whole afternoons out on a rowing boat,' she'd told them, 'catching crabs for supper.'

The idea of sticking your hand into the water and somehow pulling out a live, wriggling crab had horrified the three girls.

There was only one reason why they were marching towards the sea, about to get into a rowing boat: they hadn't been able to come up with an excuse good enough to persuade Lorelei not to hire the stupid, stinking thing.

Look at it! Gina couldn't help thinking as Logan

pulled it off the trailer and down to the water's edge. It looked ancient.

'You get in, girls,' he instructed. 'I'll take you out far enough to be floating and you can take it from there.' The amused little smirk on his face suggested that he wasn't sure if they really could.

The boat was made of absolutely plain, unadorned wood. There were two wooden benches inside for seats and a metal hook on each side for the oars to rest on. That was it.

'OK, in you get,' Logan told them – *twinkle, twinkle, little smirk* – as he watched first Gina, then Paula, and finally a very reluctant Maddison wobble and stumble into the rowing boat. The lifejackets made them all so big and bulky that it was hard for them not to bump and rub against each other all the time.

Without any consultation, Gina took one oar and Paula took the other. Gina wondered how on earth they were going to row together if they weren't even speaking.

'OK, push off.' Logan was up to his knees in the water now, but he was wearing thigh-high wellington boots as protection against the waves, which jiggled the boat up and down.

Maddison was pulling a face. She obviously didn't like this one bit. After the amount of puking she'd done on the ferry, who could blame her?

'Go on!' Logan urged when Gina and Paula just held onto the oars uncertainly, not sure what do with them. 'Reach forward, pull back – try and keep the oar in the water,' he added when Paula's flipped out and nearly smacked him in the eye.

Paula and Gina had to pull together, synchronizing their movements. For a few minutes they battled with the little waves on the shoreline and bumped up and down in the water, and Gina wondered if they would ever be able to do it. It was too hard. It wasn't like being on a pedalo in the park, that was for sure. And it wasn't anything like riding the waves on a speedboat on a bright sunny day in California either. Here, the sea was cold and grey; the boat was small and old and creaky. Gina didn't even want to think about falling out into that water. But she couldn't help thinking about it. No doubt this was all great fun in July or August, but this was November!

Gina pulled and pushed, rowing hard, staring into the water so that she didn't have to look at her friends and think about last night's argument – although she couldn't stop thinking about that either.

'You enjoying yourself yet?' Paula asked. The question seemed to be directed at Maddison, so Gina didn't reply.

'Oh yeah!' Maddison replied, heavy on the sarcasm.

'Yeah . . . riding in some dumb wooden boat in the freezing cold, wearing some dumb lifejacket – tell me, what's not to love?'

Gina's rowing began to speed up with annoyance and her mouth drew into a tight little line. Her LA friends just weren't going to get over this, were they? Maybe they were both too jealous of her new friends and her new life.

'This is so dumb,' Paula grumbled. 'This is so dumb-ass dumb. Where is the fun? Excuse me – can someone please explain? Where is the fun?'

'*Shut up!*' Gina exploded in fury. Just when her mother had finally thrown away her phone and got into the holiday spirit, these two spoiled, selfish brat-girls were about to spoil the entire holiday.

She stopped rowing and turned on her 'friends'. '*Shut up*, you whining moaners! Just stop it. My mom has brought you over here; my mom has hired the car, paid for the cottage, hired the boat . . . Would it kill you to be grateful just for one tiny little moment?'

Maddison and Paula, who had now stopped trying to row, stared back at Gina in silence.

No one said anything. They all just glared at each other in their fat lifejackets and bobbed up and down wordlessly in the little boat.

'Let's forget about this and head back,' Gina

snapped, and with that she tugged hard on her oar, trying to turn the boat towards the shore.

Suddenly the wind picked up, and a big wave came towards them; it snatched the oar out of her hand, out of the hoop, and, with a splash, dropped it into the water!

'Oh!' Gina exclaimed in surprise, and reached out to get it.

Too quickly!

She rocked the boat, startling both Paula and Maddison. There was another splash, and Gina realized that Paula's oar had fallen in too.

'For goodness' sake!' she yelled in frustration. 'Get it!'

Paula leaned right over the edge of the boat, and Maddison, who knew nothing about boats – except that she'd rather not be in one – moved to the side and reached out towards the oar too, thinking she was helping.

Gina felt the boat tip dangerously, but before she could shout any words of warning, another wave hit her side of the boat and gave it a final push.

In slow motion the boat tipped over: arms were flailing, there were shrieks of panic, but there was nothing they could do to stop it.

Then came several long, terrible, tumbling moments.

Gina felt the cold and the dark take hold of her. She was in right over her head. She spun round in the water, in the grip of an icy, sandy washing machine. Something bumped the back of her head – she wasn't sure if it was the oar or the boat. Her only thought was: *Please don't let anything bad happen to us!*

Then, with a gasp, her head broke the surface again and she was bobbing about in the water. Her wet, salty hair was plastered across her face, making it hard to see what on earth was happening. She scraped the hair out of the way with hands that felt frighteningly cold and stiff. She could see the upside-down boat; then, with a gurgle, Paula surfaced.

'Where's Maddison?' Gina shouted anxiously. She tried to kick her legs, wriggle her arms – anything to get moving so that she could go and look round the other side of the boat.

'Maddy?' she called, but with water lapping about her head and her teeth chattering madly, it didn't come out nearly loud enough.

With huge effort, Gina swam towards the rowing boat and got hold of it. She pulled herself up so that she could look over the hull. There was Maddison on the other side, looking terrified.

'Maddy!' Gina called to her. 'Thank goodness you're OK. Get hold of the boat!' she instructed as Paula came up beside her. 'I don't think Logan would like it if we lost it.'

Maddison paddled and scissor-kicked towards them until she too could grab hold of the wooden hull.

For several seconds they all stared at each other, pale, tense and frozen.

'A bit colder than Venice Beach, isn't it?' Gina asked.

It was such a silly question that it made Paula and Maddison giggle.

'I can't believe you dropped your oar as well!' Gina told Paula.

'Dropped my oar? At least I'm not the dunce who pulled the whole boat over!' Paula said, glaring at Maddison.

'Yeah, like that's going to matter when we've frozen to d-death,' Maddison managed to stammer.

'My m-mom,' Gina reminded them, 'and L-Logan. They'll get us . . . I think it takes half an hour for h-hypothermia to set in.'

'R-r-reassuring,' Paula answered. 'I'm so cold, I think I might turn C-C-Caucasian,' she joked. 'You guys are *blue*.'

'N-n-no-o-o.' Gina's teeth were chattering so hard, she could hardly get the word out. 'I always wash my hair in the Sc-c-cottish sea, so r-r-r-refreshing.'

'My hands are so c-c-cold, I can't h-h-h-hold on any more,' Maddison wailed.

'You can!' Gina insisted. 'I can hear a boat!' she added, wondering if she was just imagining it. But no, there was definitely a buzz – the buzz of an efficient, modern engine racing towards them.

'Hold on!' she encouraged Maddison. She instinctively knew that it was better for them to be together, with the boat, than for Logan to have to pick people up from all over the place.

With a disgusting blast of diesely smoke and a big splattering smack of wave in their freezing faces, a big white motor launch came bobbing alongside them. Only Logan was on board.

'Girls!' he exclaimed. 'I never expected this to happen!'

They let Maddison scramble in first. Her arms and legs were so cold and stiff that it was hard for her to climb across. Gina and Paula pushed at her with hands so numb they couldn't feel anything any more.

Paula went next – but only after a mini argument with Gina: 'You go . . . No, you . . . No, really, you.'

'Maybe the manners can wait until you've recovered from hypothermia,' Logan suggested.

He hauled Paula up first, then Gina.

In only a few moments he had tied the rowing boat

to the back of the launch. But during those moments, the three girls lying in the back of the motorboat began to feel seriously cold. They were soaked through, their hair was sodden, and it was November.

Gina's ears and cheeks were so painful, she felt as if there was a metal vice around her head. She couldn't feel her hands and feet at all. In fact, from her elbows and knees down, it was as if she was made of rubber.

The girls looked at each other as the engine roared into life again and they began to hurtle towards the shore at breakneck speed, bouncing over the waves.

'Just like surfing,' Maddison whispered, and closed her eyes.

'OK, let's keep talking, let's keep moving,' Logan shouted at them. 'No dozing – clap your hands, jiggle your feet. C'mon, we're nearly there.'

The three girls tried to follow his instructions, but their arms and legs were numb and useless.

On the beach, it all became a little blurry. Gina felt as if she was fighting the most overwhelming tiredness. It was only the chattering of her teeth and the shaking of her freezing body that seemed to keep her awake.

They were all bundled, carried and half dragged into the car, which Lorelei had waiting, engine running, right at the water's edge. The heating was already blasting out at full strength.

Lorelei and – *eek!* – Logan, stripped them to their underwear, then wrapped them in rough towels, woolly, hairy blankets and even a piece of tarpaulin from the boat shed.

Gradually the blasting heat in the car began to revive them.

'Tea!' Logan insisted. 'We need to get everyone drinking tea,' and he hurried off to his shed to brew up a pot.

As the warm liquid hit the pit of her stomach, Gina felt herself reviving a little. She opened her eyes and took a look at each of the girls bundled up beside her.

'You look like a baby owl,' she told Paula.

'An owl?' Paula replied. 'I wish I was a dolphin. I might have enjoyed that swim.'

'Or a penguin.'

'Let me know next time we're swimming,' Maddison piped up. 'I'll bring a wetsuit and a radiator.'

The best thing about the drive back to the cottage was the warmth Gina could feel on either side of her. The heating was blasting out, the tea was warming her from the inside out, but it was the two bodies pressed against her that made her feel really warm.

What if something terrible had happened?!

Imagine if Paula or Maddison had been knocked out by the boat, or trapped under it . . . or hadn't been able to survive even the ten minutes or so they'd spent in the water? Imagine if they were rushing to hospital right now, trying to reach A & E in time – though now she came to think of it, there wouldn't be a hospital anywhere near . . .

Gina leaned first to one side and then the other. 'Sorry,' she said gently against each wrapped and bundled head. 'Not just for the boat trip, but for . . . you know.'

'Yeah, me too . . .' Maddison told her.

'You know we didn't mean it,' Paula added. 'Not really.'

'Neither did I,' Gina said. 'Not really.'

'We've wasted a whole load of time,' Maddison commented.

'Yeah. Think of the fun we could have been having here instead.'

'It starts right now,' Paula promised. 'Well, just as soon as I've got this scratchy old blanket off my butt.'

Chapter Sixteen

'Amy! Niffy! Hi!'

Gina and Min, who had arrived back in Iris dorm first after half term, welcomed their friends, both struggling under a heavy load of luggage.

'The wardrobe's been moved out into the hall to make room for Niffy's bed,' Min told them. 'So you don't have to argue about who gets the top bunk,' she joked, not realizing for a moment that the pair were already locked in a much more serious argument.

Amy put one of the large holdalls she was carrying down on Niffy's bed and moved the other along to her own.

As Niffy hadn't come to school for the first half of term, she was carrying another two large bags crammed with uniform, shoes, sports kit and spare clothes.

The journey from Blacklough Hall, and then from the cab to the dorm, with all these bags had been exhausting. But through it all Niffy had refused to speak to Amy. Finally Amy had given up trying. She was not going to be forgiven for her three big crimes: playing a prank involving Ginger; not coming to the swimming pool; and, worst of all, Amy suspected, getting involved with Finn.

She *was* definitely involved with Finn – as his good-bye kisses and instructions to phone and email him asap had made clear.

'How was Blacklough?' Min asked straight away. 'I bet it was a lot more fun than my auntie's house.'

'We had a great time,' Amy said casually, turning away to unpack her bag. 'What about you, Gina?' she added quickly. 'I want to hear all about your adventures.'

'Have your mum and your friends left?' Min wondered.

'Yeah – they should be in London by now, and they catch a flight home tomorrow morning.' Gina sounded just a little bit sad. 'We had a great time. My mom really got into it – she showed us all the places she used to go when she was small. It was such good fun.'

'What did the pool princesses think of Colonsay?' Amy asked.

'Oh, they *hated* it at first – we had this huge, huge fight. I thought we were never going to talk again. It was so awful!'

Gina didn't notice Amy and Niffy's strange expressions at this piece of news.

'But then we all fell out of this boat – and somehow, after that, we were best friends again.'

'Ha!' Niffy sounded incredulous.

'No, really,' Gina insisted.

'Dermot . . . ?' Min asked. 'How did it go with Dermot?'

'Ah . . .' Gina rolled her eyes. 'I don't think Mom was quite in the holiday spirit when we met him, so it wasn't great. We might have to do that again some time and maybe it'll go a bit better.'

'Yeah, well, it's always difficult when the people you're close to don't get who you are dating,' Amy said pointedly.

'Very . . .' Niffy answered. Plucking her toilet bag from her suitcase, she went to put it in the bathroom.

'Erm . . . is something up with you two?' Min asked Amy once Niffy was out of the room.

'Oh, boy!' Amy replied. For a moment she put her head in her hands; then, looking up at her two friends, she said quickly, 'Niffy's not speaking to me. Her brother Finn – well, Finn and I played a bit of a mean trick on her . . . That's one reason—' She broke off abruptly, not sure if she wanted to go on.

'Yes?' Gina asked, understanding immediately that this wasn't the whole story. The really big reason was still to come.

'Then there's the fact that . . . well . . . I think I might actually be' – even though Amy knew it was upsetting Niffy, she couldn't help smiling – 'dating Finn!'

'Really?' Gina said.

'And Niffy isn't pleased?' Min asked.

'She doesn't seem to be, no,' Amy told them. 'Honestly, I've apologized about the trick, I've tried to find out why she's so annoyed, but she won't say a word—'

The door swung open again and Niffy came back into the room and strode over to her bed.

Min, Gina and Amy all looked up at her a little guiltily.

'Talking about me?' she asked them sharply.

'Well, we guessed there was something not quite right . . .' Min began tactfully. 'We want to help – if we can.'

Gina nodded.

Niffy turned her back on them and began to haul hockey boots out of her bag. 'Just as soon as Amy stops messing with my brother, I'll start talking to her again. It's simple.'

'I'm not *messing* with your brother!' Amy insisted angrily.

'Oh, really.' Niffy turned to glare at her. 'The day before half term you were crying your eyes out because Jason didn't like you as much as you liked him. Now, suddenly, I'm supposed to believe that you're only interested in Finn. You're just a big fat flirt, Amy McCorquodale. You can't be trusted around boys, and I don't want you anywhere near my brother. D'you understand?'

With that, Niffy turned her back on all three of them again and busied herself with unpacking.

After that outburst, all that could be heard was the sound of four girls opening and closing drawers and zipping and unzipping weekend bags.

It was horrible, Gina thought to herself. Niffy and Amy had to get over this – otherwise dorm life was going to be hell.

An almost entirely silent five minutes later, she decided that she could at least talk to Min. Hopefully that would be a neutral thing to do.

'The Gecko . . .' she threw in Min's direction. 'Have you had any word from him? He was so sweet.'

Min turned to Gina and gave her a shy smile. 'Well

. . . I checked on the computer downstairs as soon as I got back and—'

'Ooooh!' Gina couldn't resist teasing. Min had only met Greg 'the Gecko' once after they'd chatted on-line, but everyone had the feeling it was the start of a little something.

'He's sent me an email suggesting we get together on Saturday,' Min confided.

'Don't tell me,' Amy chipped in. 'You're going off to do your homework together?'

'Amy!' Min shushed her. 'He's asked if I'd like to meet him at the Natural History Museum. And he's called Greg – and can we not go on and on about how we met on the Internet?! I mean, I wasn't on-line dating or anything. It was a physics club.'

Amy and Gina couldn't help laughing at this.

'Who joins a physics club?' Amy had to ask.

'Well, people like Min and the Gecko – sorry, Greg – who are obviously perfect for each other.' Gina rolled her eyes.

'So, Min, when are you meeting him?' Amy asked.

At this there was a knock at the door, and before anyone could say anything, Mrs Knebworth strode in.

'Meeting whom, Asimina?' she boomed in her deep, window-rattling voice. 'A *boy*?!' She looked entirely disapproving.

'Erm . . .' Min cast her eyes down in embarrassment. The thought of having to discuss this with her
friends was bad enough; having to discuss it with the
Neb was terrifying.

'A *boy*, Asimina Singupta?' Mrs Knebworth
sounded horrified. 'I know that our Californian friend
Gina has a boyfriend. I know the bunch of flowers that
arrived for Amy before half term was from a certain
young gentleman. But, Asimina, I never thought I
would have to keep my eye on *you*!'

Min's gaze was fixed on the floor – Amy couldn't
think when she'd seen her friend look so embarrassed.

'Well, please tell me about this boy,' the Neb
insisted.

Min didn't say anything. She just looked as if she
wished the ground would swallow her up.

'Do your parents know about him?'

Min shook her head slowly.

'No, I didn't think so. They would not approve of
anything that might distract you from your studies,
would they, Asimina?'

Min shook her head again.

'Hang on a second' – Amy decided to wade in on
her friend's behalf – 'this is a physics geek we're talking
about here, Mrs Knebworth! They met through an
on-line science club.'

'*On-line!*' the Neb practically shrieked. 'You can't go out with boys you meet on-line, Asimina!'

'We've met him too.' Amy rushed to defend her friend. 'Min didn't go to see him on her own.'

Now Amy was pitching headlong into tricky territory. Min *had* gone to meet the Gecko on her own at Halloween. It was only because Gina and Amy had gone in search of her that they'd happened to bump into them both.

'They're planning to meet in a museum!' Amy said, exasperated. 'Does that sound dangerous to you, Mrs Knebworth? A look round the fascinating botanical exhibits and maybe a mug of tea in the café afterwards?'

'Amy!' The housemistress gave her a glare. 'There's no need to be cheeky. Anyone would think I was born yesterday. I know boys,' she said darkly. 'If you are planning to go out with this boy, Asimina' – another glare of disapproval – 'then he will have to come to the boarding house to pick you up. He will have to meet with my approval before you go off anywhere with him.' She looked at Min over the rim of her spectacles. 'I don't think your parents would expect anything less of me. Would they now?'

Min didn't give much more than a mumble in reply.

'Luella, welcome back,' the Neb said next, as warmly as she could – which was just about luke-warm. 'I'm so pleased to hear that your mother's doing well.' And with that she wished them goodnight and left the room.

'Poor Min!' Amy exclaimed. 'What are you going to do?'

Chapter Seventeen

'Welcome back, girls!' trilled Mrs Pennington, the Upper Fifth B form teacher, as she came into the classroom and strode briskly over to her desk. 'Did we all have a lovely half term?'

Amy and Niffy, both staring fixedly ahead, didn't say a word.

'Luella!' Mrs Pennington said, catching sight of Niffy. 'We're all very pleased to see you back. Such good news ... How about you, Gina? Did you go somewhere nice?' she continued chattily.

'Yeah ... umm ... my mom and some friends ...'

Gina heard the little suppressed snigger which the word 'mom' seemed to have caused. Good grief, she was American. So what? You'd think people could get over it. But some of the girls in this class were so awful. If anything was just the slightest bit different from what they expected, they pounced on it. They were just downright cruel.

Gina shot a glance at Penny Boswell-Hackett – the snidest and cruellest of them all. Penny was the worst St Jude's girl of the lot. Sometimes, the way Penny behaved, you'd think she *owned* the school. Penny thought of herself as a true Edinburgh blue-blood.

Her mother, her grandmother – even her great-grandmother – were St Jude's girls. Maybe it wasn't their fault that Penny was a revolting snob, but that's just exactly what she was. Penny and Amy had decided they were mortal enemies years ago – which meant that Gina, Niffy, Min and anyone else friendly with Amy were always viewed with suspicion by Penny and her gang.

'My *mom*,' Gina repeated, with emphasis, 'and two friends of mine came over from California and we went to Colonsay, in the Hebrides.'

'How lovely,' Mrs Pennington said with a smile, then turned to the whole class. 'And have we all met the new girl yet?'

Gina looked around the room. It wasn't so long ago that the term 'new girl' had referred to her, so she was startled to think it was now someone else's turn.

She had been so caught up with the Niffy-and-Amy huff that, although she'd said hello to a few day pupils as she'd come into the classroom before the bell, she hadn't noticed the new girl – who was sitting in the front row.

'This is Peta Sorensen,' Mrs Pennington told them. 'She's from Gothenburg in Sweden and she's with us until Christmas. I hope you'll all make her feel welcome. She's here as part of an exchange pro-gramme and she's staying with Penny Boswell-Hackett.'

Poor old Peta . . . Gina stared at the back of the new girl's head. She had the longest, lightest blonde hair Gina had ever seen. It wasn't golden blonde, like her own hair, or yellow blonde like Amy's; this was the finest, whitest hair – not colourless, not dull, but silky and shiny looking, as if it had been spun from some magical silvery metal.

As Gina considered the hair, she wondered if Peta's face could ever be as pretty. She also thought about the lines she'd written in her play, *Seeing Scarlett: Scarlett's hair was the fairest, blondest hair anyone could humanly have.*

Before Gina had even seen Peta's face, she was wondering if the Swedish girl might be interested in playing Scarlett. Mrs Parker, the English teacher, had told Gina before half term that the audition lists would be pinned up on the English department notice board today.

As the class got up and headed towards the hall, where they would join the rest of the school for assembly, Gina caught a glimpse of Peta's face. Yes! With its golden tan and fine features, it was just as stunning and perfect as her hair.

'I bet you're thinking what I'm thinking,' Amy said, catching up with her in the corridor.

'What?' Gina wondered.

'You're thinking: can that girl act? Aren't you? Because if she can, she's going to be Scarlett in your play, isn't she?'

'Umm . . . well . . . no.' Gina decided on a little white lie. 'I thought *you* wanted to be in my play. You have to try out for it, because I think you'd be great.'

She said this because she knew that Amy was just dying to be in the play.

'Duh!' was Amy's response to this. 'I don't want to be Scarlett, I want to play *you*!'

'You mean Stella?' Gina said, trying to ignore the tingle of a blush moving up from her neck.

There was just one problem with having written a play 'very loosely' based on something that had happened to her . . . Well, it hadn't in fact happened, but at the time, she'd sort of thought it had. But anyway, the problem was, everyone seemed to be talking about *Seeing Scarlett* as if it was simply a slice out of Gina's life with the names changed.

'Yeah, Stella,' Amy said with a wink.

'You know the play isn't about what really happened,' Gina said, sounding a little annoyed. 'You know Dermot wasn't seeing anyone else: I was just jealous and I made the whole thing up.'

'Yeah, I know that,' Amy said, but she didn't sound entirely convincing.

'How's your little play coming along then, Gina?' a voice asked in a familiar mocking tone. 'Are all your romantic secrets going to be laid bare on the St Jude's stage?'

Penny was suddenly beside them, listening in, ready with her spiteful little comments.

'At least she wrote it all by herself and didn't copy anyone else's work,' Amy answered for Gina, giving Penny a superior look. Aha! Considering this was exactly what Penny had done, she knew she'd got just the right dig in there.

'And Amy's got her little friend back from the country. How nice.' Penny was now referring to Niffy. 'How lovely. Cosy little chats in the dorm together again.'

Well, Penny was totally wrong there, but Amy certainly didn't want her to know that she and Niffy had fallen out. She would seize on it and never let it go. If she got involved, whatever chance Niffy and Amy had of being friends again would be ruined.

'Yes, very cosy, thanks,' Amy snapped straight back. 'At least I've got real friends and don't have to suck up to every visitor who ever sets foot in this place.'

Penny stood still, her mouth open in a little 'Oooh' of surprise.

Then Niffy totally and absolutely ruined everything by sauntering along in her casual, slouchy way and saying: 'Don't know what you're talking about, Amy. You know we're not friends any more.'

Which made the 'Ooooooh' of Penny's mouth grow even bigger.

'How *could* she? How could she have done that in front of Penny? I can't believe it!' Amy was still fuming about Niffy's comments three hours later during the lunch break.

Although Gina wanted to stay well out of this horrible argument, Amy was clearly trying to claim her as a new best friend, she thought. Amy had immediately taken the seat next to Gina's in all the morning classes, which left Niffy heading for the other side of the room. Throughout the lessons, Amy kept checking who Niffy was sitting beside and talking to. It was obvious to Gina that Amy was jealous, whereas Niffy didn't seem to care in the slightest. In fact she was trying to make it look as if she was having a great time hanging out with day girls Caitlin and Eve.

As they walked down the corridor past the English department now, Amy grabbed Gina's arm and gasped, 'Oh my goodness! There's the board. Do you think it has the auditions list up already?'

They both stopped and turned to look up at the big English department notice board. Their eyes scanned quickly over trip information, reading lists, until . . .

'There!' Amy's hand shot forward, finger pointing. Gina's eyes followed.

SEEING SCARLETT

A PLAY BY GINA PETERSON, TO BE PERFORMED

ON 10 DECEMBER

TWO SPEAKING PARTS AVAILABLE

ALL INTERESTED, PLEASE SIGN BELOW:

Two names had already been added underneath.

Gina and Amy moved closer to try and make out who it was.

'I don't believe it!' Amy said as soon as she realized whose signatures she was looking at.

Peta Sorensen was the name at the top of the list, followed by *Penny Boswell-Hackett.*

Chapter Eighteen

'OK, Amy.' Mrs Parker smiled encouragingly. 'Have a read through, and then, in your own time, deliver the speech.'

Amy looked down at the sheet of paper in her hand and saw that it was shaking. This was it: her big moment to persuade Mrs Parker and Miss Grieg, the other member of the English department, that they should definitely give the lead part in Gina's play to her, and not to any of the other girls waiting for their moment to shine.

But now that it came down to it, Amy felt a rush of nerves she'd not expected. Her hands were trembling; even her knees felt a little shaky and her throat seemed to have gone all scratchy and dry.

She stared at the words and tried to make some sense of them; tried not to let them jump and scramble in front of her eyes.

'Take your time,' Mrs Parker said kindly. 'Make sure you do yourself justice.'

The breath in Amy's chest seemed to go in and out a little too quickly for comfort.

Mentally, she rehearsed the lines that Gina had written. Gina had already let her read the whole play through. It was all about Stella who, convinced her boyfriend was cheating on her, began to do really silly, desperate things to try and find out the truth. In the play, the boy was cheating with a mysterious and beautiful girl called Scarlett. But Stella managed to pull a fantastic trick on them to get her revenge.

Any looked carefully at the words in front of her:

What do you mean you're not going to be around on Saturday? Where are you going to be? Is there something going on that I don't know about? If there is, I think you better tell me. I think it would be better for all of us if you just told me what was going on. You can't just expect me to hang around waiting for you to decide when it's convenient to fit me into your timetable. Adrian, is there someone else? Are you seeing someone else on Saturday? Because if you are, I think you should just tell me.

As Amy read through the speech, she thought about Jason.

She had been just as obsessed with oh-so-heartbreakingly handsome Jason as Stella was with Adrian. She had devoted so much time and energy to chasing that prat! Yes, he'd been utterly gorgeous and charming, whenever it had suited him – but he'd not thought there was anything the slightest bit wrong in having another girl on the side. In fact he seemed to feel that Amy was the one with the problem!

Oh! Amy felt a flush of shame and anger at the thought of his stupid little speech to her. Why had she wasted weeks of her life trying to get him to call or email or have coffee with her? If only she'd faced up to it and asked him these questions much, much earlier.

But then she understood how hard it would have been; how embarrassing and awkward. She'd have had to blurt them out, just like poor Stella.

Without giving it another thought, Amy launched straight into performing Stella's speech out loud.

She blurted, she blushed and she stumbled, just like she knew Stella would have. It must be so hard to confront the boy you're totally mad about with that question: has he really found someone else? Does he really not like you as much as you like him? Ouch. The pain of hearing this – of dreading to hear it, but of needing to hear it.

Somehow Amy was still thinking of all these things as she read out the speech, and she managed to blot

Mrs Parker and everything else in the classroom right out of her mind.

When she'd finished, she looked up, and was slightly surprised to see where she was. There was a smile on Mrs Parker's face and Amy felt a rush of excitement. She'd done well! She knew she'd done well. This was acting, and it was fantastic!

She couldn't help smiling. 'How was that?' she asked. 'It's only my first go,' she added quickly. 'There are some things I'd want to do differently – next time.'

'Yes, that's fine . . .' Mrs Parker told her. 'There are some other girls I need to see. But thank you very much, Amy.'

With that she was ushered out of the door.

Amy looked at the ten eager faces turned in her direction hoping they were going to be called in next. Her eyes fell on Peta, with her hair pulled back in a flaxen plait. Amy gave her a friendly smile, but for some reason Peta didn't smile back. She just smoothed over her hair with graceful hands.

Clearly Penny had already got to her. Well, if she wanted to be friends with Penny instead of her, that was her loss. Just so long as Penny didn't get the part in the play . . . that just couldn't happen. Amy could cope if she was beaten to the part by Peta, but Penny? No. No way.

* * *

'When are you going to find out?' Min asked when they met up later in the changing hut before the afternoon's hockey lesson.

'I don't know – in a few days, I think,' Amy replied, letting her green St Jude's skirt fall to the floor and pulling on her hockey 'skort', the strange mini-skirt/shorts kind of thing required for games lessons. She had to breathe in to do up the button. She thought of Niffy's nasty remark – but it was true, she did need to play more hockey.

'Oh, Amy!' Gina chipped in, guessing what they were talking about. 'It would be so cool if you got the part in my play. I don't want anyone else to have it!'

Amy smiled, but her attention was suddenly on Niffy.

Over on the far side of the hut, Niffy was sitting on a bench by herself, lacing up her hockey boots.

Niffy was really good at hockey – so good that she had a place in the Scottish under-seventeen team, along with Penny B-H. Min and Amy had tried out for the squad, but they hadn't managed to get a place.

Usually, during hockey lessons at school, Niffy, Amy and Min played together, side by side. They were always on the same team. Niffy and Amy played up forward; Min, who was very fast, was on the wing.

Gina, who was new to hockey and not really any good yet, tried to stay out of the way in defence. When the attackers were good enough, like Amy, Niffy and Min, there was never much work for defenders.

'So now that you're back, are we going to be in our usual positions?' Hilary, the goalie, was asking Niffy.

Amy, Gina and Min suddenly found themselves straining to hear the answer to this question. How was Niffy going to play in a team with Amy if they weren't even talking?

'Erm . . . haven't given it much thought,' Niffy replied shortly, her eyes firmly fixed on her hockey boot.

'OK. Everyone ready?' Miss McKay stuck her head into the hut. 'It's a bit nippy out there,' she told them, 'you might need tracksuits.'

Gina had already pulled on her tracksuit bottoms instead of her skirt, but she could see that Amy, Niffy and a few others were determined to brave the steely November afternoon with bare legs. It was a matter of pride to wear your skort instead of tracksuit trousers. It meant you intended to play hard enough to keep the cold at bay.

The teams began to fan out across the rough, muddy playing field.

'Luella, great to see you! Your team has missed you

sorely. Everyone in their usual positions to start,' Miss McKay instructed. 'Then I'll move you about as the game progresses. Luella, that's you playing forward beside Amy, just like before. She'll be thrilled to have you back.'

Ha!

'Usual positions' meant Niffy, Amy and Min in attack, together with Gina, Hilary and the others who made up their eleven. It also meant Penny B-H and her gang in attack on the opposing team.

With a blast of the whistle, the hard white ball was in play and the girls were charging around, wooden sticks at the ready, trying to smack it about the field.

Soon Niffy had the ball and was rushing up the pitch in the direction of the goal, but Penny was approaching fast, determined to take the ball away from her.

'Over here – pass!' Amy called out automatically – it was what she would have done in any normal game of hockey.

But Niffy blanked her. Didn't even turn her head – didn't make the slightest sign that she'd heard her – and instead passed to Min.

The first time it happened, Amy was prepared to let it go. Maybe it had been some sort of mistake, or maybe Niffy had thought it was better to pass to Min at that point.

But the next time Niffy ignored her and failed to pass the ball, Amy knew that the snub was deliberate.

Because Niffy hadn't passed, Penny swooped down to tackle her, scooped the ball up with her stick and began to race towards their goal.

'She's going to score!' Amy hissed at Niffy. 'She'll score and it will be all your own stubborn, selfish fault.'

Moments later, Penny was high-fiving her team-mate Louisa: together they had outsmarted Gina, Willow and Hilary, and sent the small hard missile whizzing into the back of the net.

'If you don't want me to be in your team, maybe I'd better be on Penny's team!' Amy hissed at Niffy again, as Penny waltzed past them, grinning smugly.

Then Niffy did something so horrible and so totally out of character that Amy could hardly believe it. With her hockey stick in her hands, she jogged over to the side line.

'Yes, Luella?' Miss McKay asked.

'Penny and I both play for the Scottish under-seventeen squad now,' Niffy began.

'Yes – how's the training coming along?'

'It's good,' Niffy answered, 'but I just thought . . .

maybe Penny and I should play on the same team at school as well. It would give us a bit of extra practice together.'

As Amy heard these words, her jaw dropped: her once best friend was going out of her way to play with her worst enemy.

Meanwhile Miss McKay smiled and agreed to the plan straight away. 'Yes, of course, Luella,' she said. 'Why don't you join Penny as a forward and I'll move Louisa over to the other team.'

Amy looked over first at Gina and then at Min. She seemed to be appealing for their help, hoping that somehow they could stop this. But Min and Gina both stared back at her helplessly.

'Are you sure, Niff?' Min called over from the wing.

'Oh yes,' Niffy said, then clenched her jaw and walked over onto Penny's side of the pitch.

Amy watched her go, and felt as if another line had been crossed. Niffy had now done something unforgiveable.

Chapter Nineteen

Amy had the part! She was really going to play Stella! Plus Mrs Parker thought that she showed 'real promise'.

She followed the path between the main school building and the boarding house and wondered why she didn't feel as excited as she'd expected to.

'*Real promise . . . real promise.*' She kept whispering the words to herself to try and kick-start the buzz she should be feeling.

She was going to *star* in a *play*. A big audience was going to see her; she was going to have lines to learn and costumes to wear. Hadn't she wanted to do this for the longest, longest time? Ever since she'd stood on the edge of the stage in the chorus at primary school?

This was a real starring role. As she trudged along, she wondered why she wasn't fizzing inside with happiness; why she didn't want to rush around and tell everyone.

And yesterday evening Finn had sent her an email: another reason to feel excited.

Gina had been on-line in the Upper Fifth sitting room, laughing over a school photo which Dermot had emailed her (captioned: *V. v. serious, v. v. short hair, collar and tie. Please forward to yr mom asap – it's my only hope*), so Amy had decided to have a little peek at her inbox. Just to see if there was anything at all from Finn. Was there a chance he'd remembered the email address she'd repeated to him seventeen hundred times or so before they'd finally said goodbye that day at Berwick station?

As soon as she'd opened her mailbox ... there it was.

To: Amy
From: FinFinNB

Hello Amy
I'm not writing anything too squishy in case this turns out not to be your email address at all. Or worse — it's your email address but your housemistress can access it (Hello, Mrs Knebworth, I think you're wonderful). Great to see you and to

get to know you a bit better. I'm
thinking of you a little too much
. . . and lots of other cheesy lines
from pop songs. Can't get you out of
my head (etc.). Lou is finally
talking to us again, so that's good.

I think we're going to be able to
meet up soon. I've put an invitation
in the post to you.

Erm . . . awkwardly struggling for
right words to sign off with:
devotedly yours? No, too formal. All
best? Noooo, too casual. Kiss kiss?
Ooooh, so babyish. I'm just going to
have to go with: Finn xx. Is that
OK?

PS. Tried to send you that clip of
you pretending to be my dad, but not
working. Will try sending to Lou's
email address. It's v. funny.

Lou is finally talking to us again . . . Amy had gone
over that line again and again in her mind. Niffy had
obviously made up with her brother, but she still
hadn't made up with her. *Far from it* . . . Amy thought
of the hockey game.

Her feelings seemed to swing like a pendulum between terrible sadness and incredible anger. Unable to decide where to settle, she was now trying to block thoughts of Niffy from her mind, but since they were in the same class, the same boarding house and the same dorm, this was just about impossible.

Now that it was all bubbling up in her mind again, Amy turned her attention to food. She was going to lose some weight. She was determined to lose some weight. She'd only had a tiny portion of lunch and was going to wait until supper before she ate anything else, no matter how many images kept floating before her eyes: chocolate cake, toast dripping with butter and strawberry jam . . .

She could hear someone running along the path behind her now, so she moved to the side to let them pass.

But then she felt a tap on her shoulder. 'Amy! I just heard! It's fantastic! It's the best!'

It was Gina, panting slightly because she'd run all the way from the school building to catch up with her friend.

'I know!' Amy plastered a smile on her face and pretended to be as crazily happy and enthusiastic as she knew she should be.

The two girls hugged, and then Gina told her that Peta had got the part of Scarlett.

'Apparently Mrs Parker had to ask the Banshee's permission,' she said, referring to the headmistress, 'because Peta's on an exchange. But Peta was so keen – plus there aren't many words to learn . . . And Mrs Parker's going to do an audition at St Lennox's to find Adrian! It is all soooo exciting.'

Gina gave Amy another enthusiastic hug. Then, glancing at her watch, she exclaimed, 'I've got to run – I promised my mom we'd speak as soon as she got into her office and I think I might already be late.'

'Yeah, fine . . .' Amy said, and waved Gina on.

'Are you going to the Duke of Edinburgh thing tonight?'

The Duke of Edinburgh!

Amy had forgotten all about it. It just didn't sound like her cup of tea at all. Some sort of awards thing where you had to learn a new skill and do voluntary work and, worst of all, climb a mountain or something. For some reason Gina had got all excited about it. Maybe she thought it would lead to meeting the Queen or something. Gina had a peculiarly American fascination with the royal family.

'Erm . . . I'm not sure . . .' Amy replied. Although

really what she meant was, I *need to find out if Niffy is going first.*

Basically, if she knew Niffy was going to be somewhere or do something, Amy made sure she avoided it. It was just too much stress. Too unpleasant.

She'd decided that at the hockey game. If Niffy was going to such lengths to avoid her that she would even play on Penny Boswell-Hackett's team – helping Penny score goals . . . it was still too utterly revolting to contemplate . . . then Amy was going to blank Niffy too.

She was going to find new friends that Niffy didn't like and she wasn't going to make up with her. Unless Niffy offered to make up first . . . obviously.

Amy pulled open the boarding-house door and was immediately surrounded by a busy throng of St Jude's girls, chatting, shrieking, scurrying off to the kitchen for the freshly baked treats that awaited them on their return (complete with the notice, totally ignored: ONLY TWO CAKES PER GIRL, PLEASE!).

Just behind the door was a little table where the day's mail was laid out by the Neb. There was never much. Almost everyone kept in touch with their family by phone or email. But still, the table always attracted a glance because there was the odd catalogue or dental appointment reminder, or the thin blue airmail envelopes from relatives of the Chinese girls.

Amy had to look twice – but yes, it was definitely her name on the envelope, in scribbly green biro, in unfamiliar handwriting.

She snatched up the letter and stared at the postmark, enjoying the guessing game, not wanting it to be over too soon. Inverness-shire? Then it was definitely from Finn. He'd written from Craigiefield, the boys' boarding school out in the middle of nowhere.

Carefully Amy tore open the top of the envelope and pulled out a postcard. On the front was a black and white photo of Audrey Hepburn. That was quite cute . . . quite tasteful. On the back, still in scribbly green biro, were the words:

Greetings to the lovely Amy . . .

Followed by the date, time and address of a party, a week on Saturday.

Underneath, Finn had written: I *really, really hope you can make it. I can't wait to see you again. Feel free to invite some of your friends along.*

Amy hugged the postcard to her chest. This was brilliant! He *couldn't wait to see her again!* How fantastic was that? Could he be any more keen? Could he be any less like the always unwilling, always elusive Jason? This was soooo exciting!

She took another look at the postcard: down at the bottom was a little arrow she hadn't noticed on the first reading, telling her to turn over.

She looked at the Audrey Hepburn photo again and wondered what Finn meant.

Then she saw the tiny writing along the side of the card: *Pls tell Nifster to come too.*

Well, that was one instruction she didn't know how to follow.

Chapter Twenty

Min curled her toes into a tight knot inside her shoes.

These were special shoes, flat and comfy but made of soft red leather with a pointy toe. They belonged to Amy, who had absolutely insisted that Min wear them on this, her very first date with the Gecko – sorry, Greg – which would finally begin just as soon as this excruciating interview with Mrs Knebworth came to an end.

Amy had, despite Min's protests, taken over her styling for this date. So she was now in the red shoes, black leggings, a pretty red and black dress which was above the knee but not so far above the knee as to give Mrs Knebworth palpitations, and a grey boyfriend jacket (also Amy's) with one of Amy's expensive hand-bags slung over her shoulder.

'I don't believe in handbags!' Min had protested. 'I'll just put my purse in the jacket pocket.'

'No, no,' Amy had insisted. 'You're having this nice

little handbag and I'm not going to take no for an answer, so shush!'

'So, Greg, where are you planning to go with Asimina this afternoon?' the Neb was asking as she made a thorough appraisal of this teenage boy through narrowed eyes.

'Erm . . .' Greg pushed his dark curtain of hair to the side nervously. His thin frame seemed to have been sucked right down into the boarding-house sofa upholstery, and Min was beginning to wonder if he'd ever manage to get out again.

Maybe she'd have to go over there and pull him out.

'We're going to the Chamber Street Museum.' Greg glanced up at Mrs Knebworth briefly, then pushed his hair out of his eyes again. She kept on looking at him as if she expected him to say more.

Instead, he felt himself shrinking shyly back into the sofa. She was scary, this lady – seriously scary.

'The museum?' she asked, raising her eyebrows and peering at him, as if her suspicions had been aroused. 'And just what are you planning to get up to at the museum?'

'Erm . . .' Greg shyly shuffled his hair about again and gave a shrug of his shoulders. 'Take a look at the exhibitions . . . maybe have a milkshake?'

'So you don't drink coffee?' was Mrs Knebworth's next question.

'Er . . . no.' Greg didn't sound too sure of himself – had he made a mistake here? Was he supposed to drink coffee? Was this a test and had he somehow failed?

'Excellent!' Mrs Knebworth suddenly smiled. 'Off you go then.' She stood up to indicate that this brief and horrible little meeting was over, before adding, 'And I'd like Asimina home in a taxi by six p.m. please. Is that OK?'

'Oh yes, of course!' Min said breathlessly, feeling a churn of nerves now that she and Greg were being directed towards the front door.

She was about to be left on her own with him!

Yes, they had chatted by email almost every day, and they had once spent half an hour on a school bench talking their heads off . . . but this was scary. She was going to be on her own with him. For hours. It was only two o'clock so she would be with him for four whole hours! What on earth would they talk about for four hours?

As soon as they were out of the boarding-house grounds, Greg turned to her and smiled. 'Phew!' he said. 'That was terrifying. I can't believe you have to cope with her all the time.'

'I know.' Min smiled back. 'I just try and keep my head down and stay out of her way.'

As they walked along the pavement together, Min felt Greg's hand brush against hers and she was so surprised – plus it was so tickly – that she pulled her hand away abruptly.

Then Greg stuffed his hand into his pocket, and that was that. They continued towards the bus stop with a gap of nearly half a metre between them.

This wasn't what Min had planned. When she'd thought about this date – and, oh my goodness, how she'd thought about it – she'd pictured them walking along hand in hand, and she'd also wondered what it would be like to kiss Greg for the first time . . . Well, in fact, kiss *any* boy for the first time. Because that was something Min hadn't done yet.

It wasn't the kind of thing you could ask people like Amy about either. She might have asked Gina or even Niffy for just a little bit of advice there, but the atmosphere in the dorm was so bad and everyone seemed in such a grump that she hadn't dared to.

So now what was she supposed to do?

She looked at Greg's hand, firmly stuck in his pocket, but it felt too stupid to say, 'It's OK, we can hold hands, you know. I didn't mean we couldn't.'

Oh . . . and now here was the bus. They'd have to

get to the museum and worry about hand-holding and kissing later.

'There's the number twelve!' she shouted. 'Run for it!'

Looking round the museum with Greg was really good fun, Min couldn't deny it. He was full of interesting stories and told silly jokes too. Her churn of stomach nerves slowed a little, but she felt a sense of sparkly excitement all afternoon long.

Every time he looked at her, every time he told her something funny or a little personal, every time she got to know a little bit more about him, Min felt a hit of excitement pulse through her.

Finally (!) she got what all the fuss was about boys: it wasn't just like making a new friend or a meeting of interested minds – there was so much more to it than that.

She *fancied* him.

There, she'd admitted it to herself. She liked the way his hair slid down against his angled cheekbone; she even liked his slouchy back and the way his stomach was so flat, his trousers seemed to sag at the front.

Every time he laughed at something she said – or listened closely and followed up with: 'Really? That's interesting, I hadn't thought of it like that before . . .' –

then she could feel her heart swell up and her head go kind of giddy in a way she didn't think she'd experienced before.

Oh yes – her first very, very big crush. It was like being at the dentist's in Durban when she was little and taking in a gulp of gas and air. It tingled and made your head swim.

'So, are you about ready for your milkshake?' Greg was asking her – but before she could answer he added, 'Do you think it was the milkshake that did it? Do you think she only likes boys who don't drink coffee? Do you think that in Mrs Knebworth's book, drinking coffee is a sign that you're a baaaaad boy?'

'Well, what about you?' Min risked. 'Are you a bad boy?'

'What does that mean?' Greg said, and leaned towards her so that their faces were only a few centimetres apart.

Then Min hesitated . . . This wasn't going to be kissing? Was it? She didn't know what to do . . .

Not wanting to risk any kind of mistake, she pulled away.

'There's a café not far from here,' she blurted out into the slightly awkward pause that followed. 'My friends are going to be there this afternoon – I wondered if you'd like to come and see them – you've met Gina before, remember?'

'Oh yeah . . .' Greg remembered her vaguely. It had all happened so quickly on that Halloween evening.

They made their way to the Arts Café – an airy, very pleasantly decorated room on the first floor of a large building that was mainly used as an art gallery. It was a café Min knew well because it was owned by the father of Gina's boyfriend, Dermot, and Dermot could be found working here most weekends. Because of this, Gina made a point of hanging out there as often as she could.

'Hi!' Gina greeted both Min and Greg enthusi-astically as soon as she spotted them. 'Over here, in the best seats!'

Gina and Niffy had indeed taken over the two leather sofas, and Dermot was just setting down two mugs of coffee in front of them.

'It's our third round,' Gina told Min. 'We're going to be buzzing.'

'No, I've made these ones decaf,' Dermot assured her. 'I'm thinking of your hearts.'

'Ohhh, you are too good to be true,' Niffy said with a wink.

'I don't deserve him,' Gina told her friends.

'No! You do not, especially after all the things your

mean mom said about me!' Dermot was quick to add.

'She did not.'

'She did too!'

'Don't worry,' Min reassured Greg. 'They're always like this. I think they love arguing.'

'Do not!' Gina said.

'Do too!' Dermot answered, then burst out laughing. 'Sit!' he instructed Min and Greg when he'd got himself under control again. 'What can I get you?'

As they looked through the menu together, Dermot took a moment to sit on the sofa beside Gina. He casually draped an arm around her shoulder, then leaned over and, without asking, casually kissed her on the neck.

Min saw. She didn't exactly mean to see; she just happened to glance up and catch Dermot's hand resting lightly on Gina's shoulder, then his lips gently touching her neck. Gina moved her head ever so slightly towards him in approval and Min felt a strange little pang. She wondered how it ever got to be so casual between people. How did you go from not being able to hold hands and sitting a careful thirty centimetres apart on a sofa to casual neck kisses? How did it begin?

Where did it go on from there?

'Tell me more about Colonsay,' Dermot urged Gina.

'How did the pool princesses cope without a mall, or a limo, or any of their other daily essentials?'

'It was an adjustment, believe me.' Gina grinned.

'And Barra?' Dermot asked. 'Did you get over to Barra and Uist as well?'

'No, we just went to Colonsay. There wasn't time to visit the others – which is a shame, because Mom knew them all well when she was little,' Gina replied.

'That's a shame,' Dermot said. 'We went to Barra at the end of the summer last year and it was spectacular. I have loads of photos—'

'You have photos?' Gina asked, leaning forward as an idea occurred to her. 'Good ones?'

'I have photos!' A light bulb was clicking on in Dermot's head at the same time. 'Really nice photos.'

'That's what you need to do then!' Gina said excitedly.

'Exactly!'

Together, Min and Niffy both had to ask, '*What?!*'

Dermot, fired up with enthusiasm, explained: 'Get Gina's mom a lovely set of photos of the islands where she used to spend her summer holidays – a nice set of three, framed, for her pure white Californian wall.'

'Yeah!' Gina agreed.

'Then Mrs Peterson is definitely going to love me,' he added.

'Ms Winkelmann . . .' Gina reminded him.

'Ah, yes, the multi-layered modern family. I am so boring – I just have one mum and one dad and one proper full brother. Boring.'

'Dermot!' came the call from across the café.

'And that will be my one and only dad now, wondering why I'm not shifting my arse fetching and carrying drinks. See ya later.' He brushed Gina's hair to the side and kissed her on the neck again.

Min saw it and felt herself blush with confusion. Would it be nice if Greg did that? She didn't know. She didn't even know!

As Dermot left to serve the other customers, Min asked, 'Where's Amy?' in spite of the reaction this might provoke in Niffy.

'She's gone out with Rosie – you know, from the year below,' Gina answered quickly, hoping this would stop any further Amy discussion in its tracks.

Then, to Gina and Niffy's glee, Greg announced that he was heading for 'the boys' room' and left the table.

No sooner was he out of earshot than the excited questioning began:

'How is he?'

'How's it going?'

'Are you guys having a good time?'

'How was the museum?'

'Do you still like him?'

'He seems totally mad about you, by the way.'

Min grinned and nodded her way through the barrage of questions, but she still wasn't prepared for Niffy's killer: 'So, have you kissed yet – on the mouth, not just that friendly on-the-cheeks "hello" stuff? Have you snogged' – she said the word with relish – 'with tongues?'

'Eeeeeek!' Min squeaked in reply.

'Uh-oh . . . Houston, we have a problem,' Niffy teased. 'Date has progressed since fourteen hundred hours and still no mouth-to-mouth contact has been established. Repeat: we have a problem.'

'Shush!' Min hissed, terrified that Greg was somehow going to overhear.

'Didn't you kiss hello?' Gina asked.

'No! The Neb was there!' Min replied.

'Oh yeah . . .'

'And later?' Niffy asked. 'Hasn't there been plenty of tonsil-tickling time since then?'

'No . . . I think . . . I think I might have blown it,' Min confided.

'Uh-oh – if you need mints . . .' Niffy offered.

'It's not that!' Min looked embarrassed, flustered even. 'I accidentally moved my hand away. I just sort of . . . got a shock,' she muttered.

'Oh dear,' Niffy said, looking sympathetic now.

'And then . . . I think he brought his face close to mine and I just sort of . . . moved . . . hesitated – I don't know. Whatever it is you're supposed to do, I think I did the wrong thing.'

'Oh, don't worry,' Gina tried to reassure her. 'I'm sure you'll get another chance. He seems to really like you. Just relax! You'll be fine.'

'Will I? It's just . . . I don't know what I'm supposed to do!' Min blurted out.

But Gina gave her a raised eyebrow look of warning. Greg was heading back towards them and it was time to change the subject.

As he sat back down on the sofa, the girls couldn't help noticing that he'd placed himself a little closer to Min, though there was still a noticeable gap between them.

After twenty minutes or so of friendly chat, it was approaching five thirty, and the girls were due back at the boarding house for supper.

'I suppose I should head off,' Greg said, giving the watch on his wrist a deliberate once over.

'Yeah . . .' Min agreed uncertainly.

'I've had a great time,' he added, colouring up at the words. 'Shall we do this again soon?'

'Yeah!' Min brightened up. 'I'd really like that.'

Greg stood up and then shook hands with both Niffy and Gina. 'Nice to see you again,' he told them.

Min stood up too and looked at her date, seized with uncertainty.

What was she supposed to do? Kiss him? *Here?!* Right in front of her friends?

'Thanks,' Min said, then wished she hadn't. Thanks for what? Duh!

Greg held out his hand to her!

He was going to shake hands!

This was all wrong!

Min gave him her hand to shake and they said their goodbyes. Then he began to walk out of the café, turning once to wave just as he reached the door.

'Go after him!' Niffy whispered. 'Go smooch on the stairs. For goodness' sake, Min, get out there. He just shook your hand! That's like the first-date Kiss of Death. *Go!*'

But Min was frozen to the spot.

Chapter Twenty-one

'OK, Peta, do you want to go through that one more time?' Mrs Parker asked briskly. 'Amy, you stay over in the corner, behind the screen. Obviously it will be a tree once we've got the props sorted out, but the screen will have to do for now.'

Amy was tired. They'd already been rehearsing for over an hour: her, Peta, Mrs Parker and the friendly St Lennox boy, Jamie, who'd been picked for the part of Adrian. Even Gina, who'd been watching for the first thirty minutes or so, had slipped away, she noticed.

Maybe Amy wouldn't have been so tired or so fed up if she felt that she was any good at this. But for most of the rehearsal, everything she did or suggested seemed to be wrong; whereas Peta ... Oh my goodness! Mrs Parker could not get enough of the wonderful, naturally talented Peta! And Jamie could barely keep his eyes off her either.

Not that Amy was interested in Jamie, obviously,

but what with him and Mrs Parker fussing and generally marvelling at wonderful, extraordinary Peta, she felt like a lumpen, untalented *frog*, croaking away from her corner behind the screen.

Once again, Peta took her speech from the top; she would no doubt deliver another flawless performance. Amy risked peeping out at her from a gap in the screen.

She was tall and thin as a whippet, with that uniquely Scandinavian complexion. Despite the soft silver halo of hair, her skin was biscuity brown and golden. She'd obviously spent the whole summer outdoors, being kissed by the northern sun. Look at those beautiful hands holding the script – although she'd already learned all her words – and then there was her lovely voice, trilling melodiously through the lines as if she'd been playing the part of Scarlett all her life.

She was such a wonderful actress – and she was so pretty . . . and so *thin*!

Amy could feel her heart sinking into her shoes. She just couldn't cope with the comparisons. Having always thought of herself as pretty and talented and thin, Amy had made an effort to dress well, get her hair cut properly, wear nice make-up. She'd always made the most of herself and thought the best of herself.

But now, as she considered the prospect of standing

up here on stage in front of the whole school beside Peta – being compared to Peta – there was no doubt in Amy's mind that she was going to be second best.

'And now Amy . . .' Mrs Parker looked at her.

Amy stepped forward and began to stumble through her lines, trying to remember all the supposedly friendly and helpful advice she'd been given on her last run-through.

Somehow, though, the more advice she got, the more confused she became and the worse her performance seemed to get.

'Not bad – much improved . . .' Mrs Parker told her.

Amy glanced over at Peta, who gave her a little smile.

It was hard to read that smile. Was it friendly? Unfriendly? Superior? Icy? Condescending? Shy? Amy didn't know. She smiled back: part of her hoped she might get to know Peta better; part of her wasn't sure she could cope.

'OK, back to your screen, Amy,' Mrs Parker said. 'We'll do that all one last time – then, I promise, I will let you go.'

Despite the dimmed lights, Amy could see two girls coming into the assembly hall and heading down towards the front row of chairs.

'Girls?' Mrs Parker turned to the pair. 'Do you have a reason to be here?'

'Peta's catching the bus back with me,' one of the girls answered.

Amy's stomach knotted at the sound of the voice. It was Penny Boswell-Hackett. Just what she needed: Penny B-H watching, comparing, taking notes and preparing choice snide remarks to insult her with later.

'Fine. Jamie? Peta? Are you ready for the final run-through?'

As Jamie started up once more, Amy peered through a gap in the screen to see who else was there with Penny.

She saw the curly dark brown hair, the pale face and the prominent nose of Penny's companion, but she still couldn't really believe it was Niffy.

What was Niffy doing here?

Why was Niffy sitting beside Penny? And *talking* to her?

Even if they did play in the Scottish hockey squad together, did Niffy really, honestly want to be Penny's friend?

Was Niffy being friends with Penny just to annoy Amy? Could that be the reason?

Amy couldn't stop watching them. Niffy was bending down – maybe she'd dropped something, maybe she was getting something out of her school bag . . .

Then she brought out her mobile phone. Amy could tell that's what it was because it glowed blue in the darkness. Even up on stage, she could hear the two girls' stifled giggles.

Niffy was showing something to Penny. Even though she had no idea what it was, Amy felt her cheeks burning. Somehow she just knew that it was something to do with her. What else could Penny and Niffy possibly be laughing about?

Was it Finn's video clip? she wondered. Had Niffy downloaded the clip – which she was now showing to Penny?!

Amy felt tears of hurt and injustice welling up in her eyes. Her throat was tightening with a lump of unhappiness.

This was too much. This was just *too* much—

'Amy!' Mrs Parker called out a little sharply. 'You've missed your cue. You were supposed to jump in there.'

With the tight dryness in her throat, Amy knew she wasn't going to be able to say anything – and anyway, she didn't want to act in front of these horrible spectators.

She quickly stood up behind the screen and felt a convenient lurch of dizziness. 'I don't feel well . . .' she murmured.

'Really?' Mrs Parker asked with concern as Amy held onto the screen for support.

'I think I'm just tired. I need to go back to the boarding house – it's nearly supper time.'

Amy knew this because she'd been checking her watch every ten minutes for the last hour. In twenty minutes it would be time for supper. She'd made it. She'd managed to last all the way from breakfast through to supper on only one small biscuit at snack time and five large glasses of water to fill the horrible rumbling empty feeling in her stomach.

Mrs Parker looked at the girls in the audience. 'Luella? Is that you?' she called out, spotting Niffy. Amy suddenly had a horrible feeling she knew what was coming next.

'You'll be heading back to the boarding house now, won't you? Can you go with Amy? She's not feeling well and I think someone should keep an eye on her as she walks over.'

Niffy shrugged. 'I've got hockey practice, Mrs Parker,' she replied.

'Well, just walk Amy back and then get to hockey – it will only take a few minutes,' Mrs Parker insisted.

Amy came down from the stage, gathered her things together and said goodnight to Mrs Parker.

Then, with Niffy following several metres behind her, she left the assembly hall.

They walked along the school corridors in silence. They went out of the main door, through the dark school grounds and onto the path that led to the boarding house . . . all in the biggest, huffiest silence.

As they went in through the gate to the boarding-house garden, Amy couldn't stand it any longer.

'What were you and Penny laughing about?' she demanded.

'What's it got to do with you?' Niffy fired back.

Amy stopped and put her hands on her hips. 'Well, that's just what I want to know. Did it have anything to do with me? I saw you – you and your new best friend Penny – having a good laugh about something, and if it had anything to do with me, then I think I should be told!'

For a moment Niffy just stared at Amy. She didn't say anything. Her face looked ready to explode with anger. But still she said nothing.

Amy couldn't take the silence. It was the silence that got to her. Amy was an arguer, a fighter; so was her dad. She wasn't used to people stomping about in great sulky silences for days on end.

'Say something!' she shrieked at Niffy. 'For God's sake will you just bloody say something?!'

'Fine,' Niffy replied in a voice which sounded too calm. 'It had nothing to do with you. It was a hockey thing. Guess what, Amy? Big news: the whole world doesn't revolve around you.'

Amy turned on her heel and headed for the boarding-house door. Suddenly she didn't have the energy to fight. She didn't have the energy for anything.

Chapter Twenty-two

'Amy!' Gina greeted her with a smile as she came into the Upper Fifth sitting room. 'Mrs Parker's finally let you go then? I was beginning to wonder.'

'Yeah – and I think she's planning my replacement,' Amy grumbled in reply.

'Don't be silly! It was your first rehearsal; you could hardly expect to be perfect,' Min reassured her.

'Peta was,' Amy said, and sank weakly down into the sofa. Just ten minutes till supper, just ten minutes to go . . .

'Peta's part is much smaller than yours,' Gina reminded her kindly.

Amy spotted the two iced cupcakes sitting on a little saucer on the coffee table in front of her. Oh, good grief – chocolate butter-cream icing, one of her favourite treats!

'I saved those for you,' Gina said, seeing where

Amy's gaze had fallen. 'If you come back late there are never any cakes left.'

'That was really kind of you,' Amy said, but then gave an exaggerated glance at her watch. 'It's only ten minutes till supper though. I'll think I'll save them for afterwards.'

'That's incredibly restrained of you,' Min said in surprise. 'They are totally delicious.'

'I know. I'll eat them . . . just later – I'd better go and put them somewhere safe, before Niffy waltzes in and demolishes them,' Amy said, picking up the little plate.

'Amy . . . ?' Gina asked, her voice serious now as she flicked a glance at Min. Together, they had both decided they needed to help Amy and Niffy make up. 'Don't you think the row with Niffy has been going on long enough? It's time for you guys to make up now. You know – maybe sit down together and talk about the whole Finn situation. Calmly. We can help you. We can ask Niffy what she thinks, if you want us to . . .'

Amy lifted a finger to her mouth and began to chew at a ragged nail.

This struck Gina as strange – she'd never noticed Amy bite her nails before.

'Niffy's not given me any sign that she wants to make up,' Amy said finally. 'I think she's enjoying it.'

'Maybe she thinks you're enjoying it,' Min said.

'Do you want us to talk to her?' Gina suggested. 'We're desperate for this to be over – it's such hard work being in a dorm with the two of you at the moment. It's really uncomfortable.'

'Yeah,' Min agreed.

'Well, what about the hockey?' Amy asked. 'She's moved to Penny's team. I saw her with Penny this evening.'

'They're in the hockey squad together,' Min said with a shrug. 'Maybe that's all it is. Maybe it's nothing to do with you.'

Amy found these words familiar. That's what Niffy had said: maybe it was true; maybe it *had* just been about the hockey.

'You're both so stubborn,' Gina said, 'but you played the trick on Niffy, you're her brother's new best friend – maybe you should try apologizing first.'

'We'll try and talk to her,' Min offered again, 'if you want us to.'

Amy shook her head. 'Look,' she said finally, 'just let me think about it, OK? Maybe you're right, maybe I'll have to say sorry first . . . but just give me a bit of time.'

Picking up the saucer with the little cupcakes, Amy got to her feet. She wanted this uncomfortable conversation to end, so she blurted out, 'I better go and put these in a safe place,' then left the room.

'OK . . .' Min said.

'Please think about it,' Gina called after her.

As soon as she was out in the corridor, Amy headed straight for the laundry room, which was usually very quiet at this time of the evening.

Switching on the light, she went over to the swing-top bin. Without hesitation, she tipped up the saucer and launched the two delicious little cupcakes straight into the rubbish.

Then she peered through the flap to see where they had landed: right down amongst the empty packets of laundry powder. Good! The temptation to eat them was over.

Amy had decided that there had to be at least one thing in her life which was under her control. Although she might never be as pretty or as talented as Peta, she could make sure she was as thin.

Back in the sitting room, Gina turned to Min. 'The cupcakes . . .' she began.

'Yeah?' Min asked.

'Have you noticed? Over the past few days . . . I think Amy's gone a bit weird about food.'

Chapter Twenty-three

School lunches at St Jude's were unusually good. There was plenty of fresh, tasty, healthy food. The slimy stews and soggy steamed puddings that girls might have had to put up with in the past had long ago been replaced by baked potatoes, adventurous salads, grilled fish and chicken, pasta dishes, and lightly steamed vegetables.

The odd member of staff was on duty in the lunch hall, keeping a watchful eye on queue-jumping, but there was no strict supervision. In the past, a teacher had sat at the head of every one of the twelve dining tables, eating with the girls and handing out detentions to anyone who couldn't get through their helping of stringy lamb casserole and boiled potatoes. Nowadays the girls were usually left to their own devices.

Gina and Min were sitting with Serena and Willow from their year and Rosie from the year below.

'Where's Amy?' Rosie asked for the third time.

'I dunno,' Gina told her. 'She said she was coming straight up, but would have to eat quickly because she had a rehearsal in the lunch break.'

'But I've been here since the bell went and I haven't seen her,' Rosie complained.

'Well . . . that's weird,' Gina had to admit. She found herself exchanging a look with Min.

Over the past few days they'd both missed Amy at lunch – only for her to claim later that she'd dashed in, wolfed something down and had somehow missed them.

'I was looking for you,' she had insisted. 'I've no idea how we didn't see each other.'

'You don't think . . .' Min began, but then she seemed to think better of it, and instead asked, 'What's happening this weekend? Is anything happening? Amy said something about a party that we were all invited to, and I thought if we were going, then I'd tell Greg to come along – because he emailed and said he'd like to see me,' she ended shyly.

'Ooooooh!' Gina and Rosie chorused together.

Then Gina started to explain: 'OK, the party – it's complicated. Yes, there is a party. Amy's going to see Finn and Niffy's going to see Finn – so that's going to be interesting . . . Unless, you never know, maybe they'll have made up by then. Maybe Finn will bring them together again. We're allowed to bring friends, so Greg can come, Dermot can come – Rosie, you, Willow and Serena and a couple of other friends can come. But we'll all have to think of a really good cover story, because let's face it' – here came the very big complication – 'the Neb isn't going to let us go.'

They all fell silent.

'Can't we think of *anything*?' Rosie asked.

'Well, Amy's suggestion was,' Gina began carefully, looking at Willow, 'if a day girl got their mom to phone Mrs Knebworth and ask if we could go to a party at their house, that might be OK.'

Willow looked at her in surprise. To a day girl, all the rules, regulations and complications of being a boarder far outweighed the hours of fun the girls must have in each other's company every evening.

'You need my mum to phone up your house-mistress and ask for you all to come over to a party at my house – are you joking?!'

'Are we joking, as in, no way your mom would do it? Or as in, you can't believe the lengths we have to go to?' Gina wanted to establish.

'I can't believe the lengths you have to go to,' Willow replied. 'I mean, it's just some flat party with some Craigiefield boys, and we'll all be home by midnight.'

'Erm ... eleven o'clock sharp, in a taxi,' Gina corrected her, and pulled a face.

'Your life is too exciting,' Willow teased, scraping the very last of the peach yoghurt from the carton in her hand.

'I know. How can we stand it?' Gina joked.

'I'm going to have to go,' Rosie said, looking at her watch. 'I've got a music lesson in ten minutes.'

'I'm heading off too,' Willow said, stacking all her lunch things on her tray and manoeuvring her legs out from under the table and over the wooden bench. 'I'll ask my mum, OK? I'm not sure what she'll say, but I'll ask her.' She headed off, followed by Serena.

Gina and Min were left facing each other over the dining table. Min was eating her way slowly and thoughtfully through a small slice of banoffee pie; Gina had already finished her two courses and was topping up her water glass to have something to do.

'What were you about to say about Amy?' she asked her friend.

'Erm ... well – her eating ...' Min hesitated.

'Have you sat beside her at supper lately?' Gina asked.

'Yes,' Min replied with a look of concern on her face.

'She asks for a small helping of the main course, then hardly touches her pudding, that's what I've seen. Every night,' Gina said.

'Yes, me too,' Min agreed.

'I haven't seen her at lunch for three whole days, Min,' Gina added anxiously. 'If Rosie says she's been here since the bell . . .' She glanced up at the grand old station clock on the dining-room wall. 'The dining room's going to close in three minutes,' she pointed out.

The friends looked at each other. Now they knew for certain that Amy was skipping lunch.

'This morning she ate one oatcake and a banana,' Min said. 'How on earth is she going to make that last till supper time?'

'My friend in California, Ria . . .' Gina began. 'Her sister's in hospital – she's really sick because she stopped eating. We've got to try and talk to Amy.'

'Gina, this is scary,' Min said. 'What can we do?'

Chapter Twenty-four

Niffy boarded the bus, hauling her large bag of hockey kit in after her. She fumbled for money, got her ticket then dragged herself and her bags along to the first available seat.

She was exhausted. It was nine-thirty in the evening and she'd been running up and down the Scottish hockey squad's training pitch for two and a half hours. She was ravenous too, but the boarding-house packed supper was long gone; she hoped she'd be able to make herself a mountain of toast as soon as she got back.

The other St Jude's girls on the squad were all day girls – who'd been picked up by a posse of parents in estate cars and 4x4s, Niffy couldn't help noticing. Every single one of them had driven straight past her as she'd trudged along to the bus stop in the drizzle. Not one had thought of offering her a lift. In fact, Niffy was sure she'd seen something like a smirk on Penny's face as she'd passed by – and the Boswell-Hackett family home was only a five-minute walk away!

Penny might have seemed friendly when Niffy had shown her the hockey-disaster video clip at the play rehearsal the other night, but the truth was, she was a cow. She pretended to be friendly one minute – if she thought there was something to be gained from it – but she'd just as likely blank you the next.

The bus stopped, and Niffy glanced up to see a tall, dark-haired boy in St Lennox uniform get on. As he paid for his ticket, she had the feeling that she'd seen him before – knew him even. She realized with a lurch who it was and quickly turned her face to the window, hoping he wouldn't see her.

But Amy's last, brief boyfriend – the famously handsome Jason – walked slowly up the aisle looking for a seat, and chose the one in front of her. Then, in his typical smooth manner, he said, 'Hello there – you're Amy's friend Niffy, aren't you?'

Before Niffy could reply, he'd clocked her tracksuit and was asking, 'Been out training? Are you with the Scotland squad? That's impressive.'

Niffy fixed him with a cool gaze. 'Hello, Jason,' she said finally. 'Yeah – under seventeens. It's really hard work though. I'm shattered.'

There was a little more small talk before Jason

finally asked the question Niffy had been expecting: 'So how's Amy? I haven't seen her since . . .'

'Halloween?' Niffy suggested.

'Yeah . . .' Jason cleared his throat. 'That didn't go so well.'

'No,' Niffy had to agree. 'I can't imagine you've heard much from her since then.'

If Jason had been any normal sort of guy, he'd have said no and maybe moved on to other less awkward topics of conversation. But Jason had an amazingly over-inflated opinion of himself. He thought he was the best-looking, most charmingly irresistible Adonis of St Lennox. He hated the idea of Amy McCorquodale telling him to get lost, in front of people he knew, at the St Jude's Halloween party. He really hated it. So what if he'd had another interested girl on the side – who could blame him? So he missed a date: he'd spent a lot of money on apologizing with flowers!

So instead of saying no, Jason leaned over, smiled slyly – and told Niffy a complete and utter lie. 'Poor old Amy,' he began. 'I think she's very sorry. She still emails me several times a week wondering if I'd like to come and meet her for a coffee. In fact, I've finally given in – I'm going to see her . . . on Sunday, I think. But don't tell her you ran into me – for some reason she wants to keep this top secret,' he added, and even winked for effect.

Niffy felt tears of rage well up in her eyes. She *knew* it! She knew Amy was never going to get over Jason in a weekend. Finn was just a tonsil-tickling distraction to while away the time while she planned her next meeting with this slime-ball.

And what about Finn? When he found out about this, he was going to be so upset . . .

Amy had thought about what Min and Gina had said for several days now. She knew that Niffy wasn't Penny B-H's new friend; in fact Niffy hadn't made any new friends at all. When she wasn't with Min or Gina, she was often wandering the corridors of St Jude's on her own. She also spent a lot of time in the dorm on her own – when she wasn't attending her two hockey practices per week . . . on her own.

So Amy had decided that when Niffy came in from hockey tonight, she would be waiting for her in the little boarders' kitchen. While Niffy made the stack of toast she'd need after an evening of training, Amy was going to try and talk to her; try to build a bridge.

Wasn't that what Finn would want? They were going to see him at the weekend, so wouldn't it be best if they tried to patch things up for his sake?

Amy waited in the kitchenette with the large bags of soft white bread and tried to work out what she was going to say to Niffy. She avoided thinking how much she would like a piece of toast. She was winning: although there were no scales in the boarding house, she could tell from the feel of her clothes that she was losing weight fast. It was just a matter of willpower. Mind over matter . . . mind over *fatter*.

The front door banged open and, with a clatter of bag and hockey stick, Niffy came in. She went into Mrs Knebworth's sitting room to sign in, then, just as Amy had predicted, headed straight for the kitchenette, where girls were allowed to help themselves to tea and toast and fruit in between meals.

'Oh, hi,' Amy said as Niffy came into the room. 'I was sort of . . . well . . . I was just hoping I might find you here and that we might be able to have . . . just . . . I don't know, some sort of . . .' Her eyes dropped to the floor.

The expression on Niffy's face was not exactly making this easy. She looked angry. What the bloody hell was she still so angry about? It was ages since the Ginger joke; ages since she and Finn had become an item. Could Niffy honestly not get over this?

'Talk,' Amy said finally. 'Try and have a talk about . . . stuff.'

'Are you joking?' Niffy stormed. She couldn't believe what she was hearing. Ever since Jason had spoken to her on the bus, she'd been wondering how to tell Amy and, more importantly, Finn, that she knew exactly what was going on.

Now that Amy was standing right here in front of her, Niffy felt unbelievably angry.

'Get out of here!' she said furiously. 'I know exactly what you're up to.'

Red in the face with anger, embarrassment and hurt, Amy fled the room. Gina and Min were totally wrong: she and Niffy were never going to be friends again in a million years!

Chapter Twenty-five

'Amy . . .' Gina began as she and Min hurried into the dorm after school, hoping they would find Amy there on her own.

She was lying on her bed, flicking listlessly through a magazine. Gina looked at her closely. She kept trying to see if Amy was losing weight, but it was hard to tell under the sludge green of the St Jude's uniform. Amy's jumper had always been long and baggy and her skirt had always slipped nonchalantly to her hips.

She looked very pale – there was no doubt about that – her cheeks chalky-white, with dark rings under her eyes. But then if Gina had to survive through till supper on one oatcake and a banana, *she'd* look pale too.

'Min and I want to talk to you,' Gina said carefully, and sat down on the end of her friend's bed.

'Oh, good grief – if this is about Niffy again, you can just forget it,' Amy muttered. 'I tried to talk to her last night and . . . Just forget it. Whatever you thought about her being ready to be friends again, well, you were completely and utterly wrong. I wish I'd never bothered. It was totally embarrassing.'

'Oh . . .' Gina sounded surprised. 'Well . . . But there's something else.'

'Not about Niffy,' said Min. She sat down on Gina's bed, which was next to Amy's.

'What?' Amy asked. 'You both look so serious!'

'Erm . . .' Gina took a deep breath and decided to just come out with it. 'You're not eating properly. You have tiny breakfasts, tiny suppers and you're not eating lunch at all.'

'It's so bad for you,' Min chipped in before Amy could reply. 'You have to stop it, or else . . . we're going to tell the Neb.'

She and Gina had decided beforehand that this was what they would tell Amy.

'Wh-what?!' Amy said with a gasp. She dropped her magazine and sat up to face them.

'We've noticed,' Gina said gently.

'We're really worried about you,' Min added.

For a moment Amy looked angry, but then she seemed to think better of it. 'You know,' she began, 'I *have* skipped lunch – a few times – and I have been trying to eat less . . .'

'Why?' Min wanted to know.

'I just feel a bit . . . chubby,' Amy admitted.

'Don't be stupid!' Gina jumped in. 'You're beautiful – and, Amy, Ria's sister is in hospital because she didn't eat. She's made herself really, really sick. Everyone over there is so worried about her.'

'OK, OK.' Amy looked almost embarrassed about their concern now. 'I won't do it any more. I'll go to lunch and I'll be normal, OK? Don't worry about it – and I don't want you to talk about it either – to anyone else.'

'Of course not,' Gina and Min both agreed straight away.

'What about the party?' Amy asked, desperate to change the subject.

'Bad news,' Gina replied. 'Willow's mum won't make the call to the Neb for us.'

'Oh no!' Amy groaned.

'I didn't think it was very likely,' Min said. 'I mean, what mother wants to get involved with lying to the school? What if something happened to us . . .? Then it would kind of be her fault. Well, she'd be involved.'

'Oh, great!' Amy gave a sigh. 'Well . . . now what are we going to do?'

Gina propped her chin up on her hands. 'How do other people get to go to parties? Who in the boarding house goes to the most parties?' she asked. 'We should speak to them and find out how they do it.'

A little smile began to grow on Amy's face. 'Mel!' she said brightly, naming the most notorious girl in the entire boarding house. 'We need to go and talk to Mel!'

Mel was the self-proclaimed 'bad girl' of the school and resident 'sexpert'. She always wore the raciest clothes she could get away with, had the most out-rageous haircut and colour the Neb could tolerate – and the dodgiest boyfriends.

The last guy she went out with (*and more*: all explicit details available to anyone who approached her room with a bribe) had been interviewed by the police for 'prowling' around the boarding-school garden in the hope of a secret meeting with her.

Mel was constantly on her last and final warning from the Neb for something or other, but she had a breezy charm and an absolutely loaded daddy, and these things had so far protected her from the ultimate punishment: expulsion.

'Oh no!' Min groaned. 'Count me out of anything that involves her. She's just undiluted trouble.'

But Amy had already hopped down from the bed and was sliding her feet into black pumps. 'C'mon,' she instructed Gina. 'I bet she has the answer for us.'

Gina wasn't quite so optimistic, but still she got up and prepared to follow Amy.

Just then, the door opened and Niffy walked in.

'Don't worry, I'm leaving anyway,' Amy snapped at her former friend. 'We're going to find a way to get to the party on Saturday. Yes, the one you're determined I won't go to. Well, too bad. I'm going there to see your brother.' There was a sneer in her voice as she said this.

'Don't!' cried Min. Amy and Niffy had once been such close friends, she hated to watch them fighting like this.

But there didn't seem to be anything that she or Gina could do to stop it.

'So Mel's got a room all to herself again?' Gina asked Amy as they approached Mel's door.

'I don't think anyone else would share with her,' Amy said. 'Imagine having to live with all her stories and horrible little details twenty-four/seven.'

'Eeeek!'

While Mel was a fascinating source of information, there was always just a little bit too much of it. Gina's toes curled at the thought of some of the squishy details Mel had provided when she'd told them about her first night of passion. Now Gina could never think about Mel without also thinking about Mel's boyfriend's horrible blue underpants. And she didn't want those underpants there, taking up room in her head. She really didn't.

'Hi!' Amy called out. 'Are you in? It's Amy and Gina.'

The door opened, and Mel ushered them into her utterly chaotic room. The bed was completely covered in outfits which she was obviously trying on in advance of the weekend. Her face looked unusual too. She'd obviously applied fake tan in far too dark a shade, along with an overdose of purple lipstick.

'Oooh' – Amy tried to stifle a giggle – 'you look like a burned blackcurrant.'

'Very funny,' said Mel, but she let them into her room and cleared a corner of her bed for them to sit on.

Then she squirted some cleanser into her hand and began to rub it across her face. 'Any tips for removing fake tan?' she asked her visitors.

'Erm . . . lots of showering and scrubbing,' Amy offered.

'Yeah,' Gina pitched in. 'If you've got one of those body brushes—'

'This is my face!' Mel protested. 'I'm not about to attack it with a body brush!'

'No, I guess not,' Gina had to admit. 'Exfoliator? I might have some if you don't.'

'Yeah, but only if you help us,' Amy jumped in. Mel never ever did anything for free – she always had to be bribed into everything, so Gina certainly shouldn't be giving away exfoliator when it could be used as a negotiating tool.

'So . . . what's the problem?' Mel asked. She sat down on the chair at her desk, crossed her legs, then placed freshly painted navy-blue fingernails on her snakeskin print leggings.

'We've been invited to a flat party on Saturday night,' Amy began.

'Oooo!' Mel sounded interested. 'A party! Can I come?'

'Of course,' Amy agreed, knowing nothing was more likely to make Mel determined to come than saying no. 'I'm not sure it's quite your scene though – lots of Craigiefield boys aged sixteen and seventeen . . .'

'Drinking beer for the very first time . . .' Mel pulled a burned blackcurrant face. 'Mmm, maybe not. It could get really messy. Promise me that as soon as the first boy pukes, you'll leave. You don't want to get involved with the whole bucket and mop operation, trust me.'

'Promise,' Amy said. 'But the problem is, it doesn't look like we'll be able to go unless we can think of something really, really good to tell the Neb. We were going to have this day girl's mum phone and say we were going to a party at her place but—'

'The mum won't oblige,' Mel chipped in with complete understanding: she'd been in this situation so many times that she now had a whole new system in place.

'OK, all I'll need is the name of your day girl's mother and five pounds from every girl who's going. Then I'll be able to sort it for you.'

'Really?' Amy brightened.

But Gina wasn't quite so easily convinced. 'Five pounds!' she exclaimed. 'Each?! And what do you mean you'll need the name of the mum we were going to get to phone.'

'It's very simple, but I'll need the cash upfront,' Mel said firmly.

Gina couldn't help thinking that Mel was probably going to be a sensational businesswoman one day. She really understood how to make a deal. And no matter what it was you wanted, she usually already had it, or knew how to help you get it.

'So what do you do?' Amy asked.

'Let's just say I have a very good friend who's a bit of an actress. For a reasonable fee, she is prepared to phone the Neb, pretend to be the mother of your choice and request the presence of your company at a small dinner party to be held in her comfortable New Town family home. How does that sound?'

'Brilliant!' was Amy's verdict.

'A bit risky?' was Gina's.

'Don't be silly.' Amy dismissed her concerns. 'C'mon, let's go and get our money, then we'll give Mel a squish of your exfoliator and we'll all be set for Saturday.'

Gina didn't look convinced, but she followed Amy out of Mel's room.

As they began to head up the staircase together, they saw Niffy coming down. She was in a hurry, taking the stairs two at a time.

Amy deliberately turned away to make it obvious that she didn't want to even see her.

Chapter Twenty-six

'Wear the cream dress.' Amy was looking at the selection of clothes Gina had laid out across her bed.

'But it's so special,' Gina protested. 'I've not worn it anywhere yet. Do you have any idea how much my mom paid for it?'

'Wear the cream dress,' Amy repeated, 'with the cute new boots and your green coat on top, and you will be adorable. Dermot hasn't even seen it yet – which is a crying shame! Show it off. It's sooo beautiful.' A true clothes connoisseur, she felt the soft woollen fabric of the dress between thumb and forefinger. 'Mmm,' she said appreciatively.

It was five o'clock on Saturday – still a whole three hours to go before they left in taxis for the flat party – but there was so much to do! Clothes and shoes had to be decided on, everyone had to approve everyone else's outfits, and then hair had to be arranged, make-up applied.

Min and Amy were jumpy with nerves, preparing to see boys they still didn't know well but were so excited about. Gina was happy: dates with Dermot were always great. The only person who had no particular reason to feel excited about this party was Niffy.

But she was coming – there was no doubt about that. She had paid her five pounds to be part of Mel's scam. Now she stomped out of the dorm armed with her towel and wash bag and headed for the shower.

Min zipped up the pretty pink sleeveless dress she'd chosen for tonight.

'That looks really nice,' Gina told her.

'Yeah!' Amy agreed. 'So you're going to put the black jacket with that and those nice black suede pumps – that'll look gorgeous. How is Greg going to be able to resist you?' she teased.

Min could only manage a faint smile in response to this.

'The big kiss,' Amy began. 'That's what we're aiming for here.'

'C'mon then: what are *you* going to wear?' Gina asked Amy, desperate to know.

'Oooooh ... did I just happen to go into town today with Rosie, and did I just happen to stumble across something really, really special which was marked down in the mid-season sale? Oh yes, I did.'

Amy went out to the small wooden wardrobe – now on the landing – opened the door, fished around for a moment, then brought out a slinky, slithery dark blue dress made of some amazing sparkly material.

'Oh, wow!' Gina said.

'Oh yes!' Amy said, and held the dress against herself. 'I've got my patent leggings and some very high black shoes which are going to look amazing with this. I think I'll put my hair up and lash on lots of blue-grey eyeshadow.'

'It's absolutely tiny,' Gina blurted out.

'I know. Size six!' Amy revealed, and there was a gleam of triumph in her eyes as she said it.

'Six!' Min exclaimed. 'I thought you were a ten.'

'Well, this is a six and it fits,' Amy said – and her smug smile made Gina feel uncomfortable all over again.

She exchanged a glance with Min.

For the last two days they had watched Amy at breakfast and dinner. She seemed to be eating normally then, just as she'd told them she would. Lunch was still the meal that was causing problems. Amy claimed she'd gone on both days, but neither Amy nor Min had seen her.

'I think I'll get dressed and go to Rosie's room

before *you know who* comes back from her shower,' Amy said.

'Oh, you can't start calling her that,' Min protested. 'It's just so stupid. How long is this going to go on for?'

Amy shrugged, then added cattily, 'You'll have to help her out on the fashion front – you know what a complete dolt she is. She's probably selected some old jodhpurs to wear tonight.'

'Amy!' Gina scolded her. 'Don't be mean about Niffy. We're never going to join in with that.'

Amy's amazing outfit raised several pairs of eyebrows. Once she was in the teeny, slinky, glittering dress, Gina and Min looked at each other meaningfully, because now they could see just how skinny she was. Her collarbones, her hips, even her elbows and knees seemed to jut and protrude.

And then, when they were downstairs, there was the Neb's comment: 'Don't you think that's a bit over the top for a dinner party, Amy?'

Both Gina and Min were suddenly worried that she was becoming suspicious.

But Amy replied breezily, 'I'm a Glaswegian, Mrs Knebworth. I have a reputation for bling to uphold.'

So nothing had prevented the four of them from leaving the boarding house and getting into the pre-booked black cab.

'I can't believe it,' Min had whispered once the taxi doors were shut. 'If we ever get found out, we are *dead*.'

'She is not going to find out,' Amy insisted. 'We are going to a dinner party. Willow's mum and dad will be there, a few other day girls and some St Lennox boys. We will have delicious roast beef with all the trimmings – mmmm, roast potatoes, carrots dripping with butter and honey – followed by' – she half closed her eyes, as if the thought of pudding was almost too much – 'lemon meringue pie. A beautiful homemade lemon meringue pie, still warm from the oven, with thick pastry and a really gooey lemony inside . . .' She paused for a moment, then briskly added, 'So we'll say it was all lovely and we had a wonderful time.'

There was a snorting sort of 'humph' sound from Niffy, who was perched on one of the fold-down seats. Her eyes were fixed on the window so that she couldn't even accidentally look at Amy. 'Shame someone told the Neb we were going to a dinner party so we couldn't even eat a proper supper before going out,' she said.

'That didn't stop you wolfing down eight slices of toast with peanut butter though, did it?' Amy snapped back.

'At least I have slightly more than a cup of tea lining my stomach,' was Niffy's reply.

'Yeah, well, some of us have a beautiful slinky dress

to fit into,' Amy snarled. 'Some of us aren't wearing our old—'

'Please stop it,' Gina broke in. 'This is really horrible. Stop it. And anyway, I think Niffy looks great.'

Which was true. Niffy wouldn't be persuaded out of her favourite, comfortable old jeans, but she had accepted the loan of a pale yellow top from Gina, who had also insisted on brushing and tying up her unruly bundle of dark brown curls and then subjecting her to blusher, lip gloss and perfume.

The taxi journey continued without any further conversation. In fact, the silence felt so oppressive that the driver piped up with: 'C'mon, girls, it's Saturday night and you're all looking lovely. Cheer up – here we are!'

There was the usual scramble in four purses to club together for the fare. Gina weighed in with a one-pound tip, which made everyone gasp, but as she reminded them, 'I'm American: I have a reputation for over-tipping to live up to.'

Outside, it was bitterly cold, dark and drizzly, with a biting wind, and looking up at the elegant three-storey block of flats in front of them, they definitely felt nervous.

Two of the second-floor windows were lit, and it

was obvious from the shadows crossing to and fro in front of them that this was where the party was happening.

'Greg said he'd be here at eight twenty,' Min told them. 'Could we just wait out here on the pavement for him? Well, I mean, I'll wait if you want to go in.'

'I'll wait with you,' Niffy offered, desperate to avoid making an entrance with Amy.

'Good idea,' was Gina's verdict; she really didn't want to see how Finn coped with meeting both Amy and Niffy at the same time. It probably wasn't going to be a very happy moment. He was about to find out how badly they had fallen out.

So Niffy and Min stayed outside on the pavement as Amy and Gina walked up the steps and looked for the right bell to push.

'Do you think Dermot's here already?' Amy asked.

'No,' Gina told her. 'He wanted me to call him when I arrived, to make sure he doesn't end up marooned in a sea of Craigiefield boys with no one to talk to.'

Amy ran her dark red fingernail up the list of names. 'Cresswell-Smith,' she said. 'This is the one.'

'Are you nervous?' Gina asked her.

'Nah!' Amy insisted. 'Excited!'

A voice on the intercom shouted a welcome and the door buzzed open. They entered a cool, stone-flagged lobby and began to climb the stairs to the second floor.

'It doesn't sound very wild,' Amy said as they reached the top flight of stairs. This was true. There was no thumping music, no raucous laughter, no flash of disco lights or anything to suggest that a party was in full swing.

'Oh no!' she worried suddenly. 'You don't think they're all sitting about pretending to be grown up, do you? We're not going to go in and find everyone sipping sherry or something awful?'

'No!' Gina exclaimed – she just couldn't imagine it. 'Surely . . . surely it would have said on the invitation?'

Amy snorted. '*Boys* wrote that invitation. Boys know nothing.'

'Amy, boys would not sit around sipping sherry,' Gina assured her.

'We are talking about Craigiefield boys here. I mean, the word *snobby* doesn't even come close.'

They were at the door of the flat now. It looked big, smart, polished – and very grown up.

'We are at the right address, aren't we?' Gina worried.

'Yeah, I'm sure we are.'

Amy rapped hard against the wood with her knuckles.

Both girls held their breaths as they waited for the door to open.

Then a boy's head appeared. He looked at the girls and grinned. 'Hi!' he said cheerily. 'I'm Max.' He held out his hand. 'You must be friends of . . . ?'

'Finn's,' Amy said, understanding at once that this was the host and he was making a polite check that they weren't gate-crashers.

'Fantastic.' Then, holding the door open, he waved them in.

The girls walked into a hallway that looked far too well decorated to be a student flat. The wallpaper was the expensively printed kind; the elegant semicircular mahogany table bore a brass lamp with a silk shade, several telephone directories and an old-fashioned dial phone.

'Is this your place?' Amy asked.

'My big sister's,' Max answered. 'She's away for the weekend and she said I could bring a friend to stay as long as I didn't have a party. So we're all on our absolute best behaviour. Is that clear?' But he shot Amy a wink.

'Right.' Amy walked along the corridor, admiring the nubbly sea-grass flooring. Poor Max, he had absolutely no idea! That stuff was impossible to clean. If anyone spilled so much as a splash of water, his sister was going to *kill* him.

'The sitting room is on your right – half the party

is going on in there. The kitchen is on your left; the other half is happening there. Give me your coats – I'll go pile them in the bedroom. I don't think anyone's partying in there . . . not yet anyway.'

Gina gave a tense smile. She didn't think that deserved the laugh he was obviously expecting.

'Some friends of ours are coming up in a minute,' she told Max. 'Luella, Finn's sister, Min and her boyfriend, Greg. I hope that's OK?'

'The more the merrier,' Max said airily.

Gina slipped her green coat off her shoulders and passed it to him, noticing his appreciative look at her cream dress and boots.

But before he could comment, Amy's silky parka was off and she was standing there in her amazing glittery blue dress and shiny leggings.

'Wow!' Max grinned. 'That is a fantastic dress. You look far too amazing for this party. Both of you,' he corrected himself gallantly. 'You both look far too brilliant for my humble flat party.'

'Oh, get away!' Amy said, and gave him a friendly pat on the arm.

She stole a glance through the open sitting-room door to check if Finn was in there. No point going in and standing around awkwardly, unsure if she knew anyone or not.

But then Finn, all six foot three of him, complete with gangly legs and arms, was in the hallway, astonishment across his face. 'Amy! Amy! You're here – you look unbelievable!'

Before she could even think about being shy, Finn put his long arms around her and was kissing her on the mouth.

It happened so suddenly, so unexpectedly . . . And what with the buzz and nerves of seeing him again, Amy felt completely dizzy and breathless.

Gina, now stranded in the hallway with the kissing couple because Max had disappeared to look after his guests, wasn't quite sure where to look. She decided to be brave and venture into the kitchen.

She pushed open the door and saw several teenagers sitting round a small table chatting animatedly. Just as she was about to blush, mumble and back out again, a boy jumped up, and to her surprise called out, 'The Yank! It's the Yank, my friends, all the way from California.'

Her heart sank. It was bloody Charlie bloody Fotheringham. How had she managed to forget that Charlie always seemed to turn up whenever Finn was around? Just like a toad from under a rock, she couldn't help thinking. He was such a sleaze-ball, always trying to sneak a feel or a quick snog. And why, oh, why did he always have to refer to her as 'the Yank'? It was just so rude.

But he'd come up to her now, giving her a slurpy kiss on the cheek and slipping an arm around her. When his hand dropped down to her butt, she quickly moved forward so that it just fell to his side.

'A glass of wine?' he suggested.

His face was too close to Gina's, way too close – she could smell his sour wine-laced breath and see how the dark red sediment had stained his teeth and sat in dark lines in the cracks of his dry lips.

'I think I'll have a Coke or an OJ please,' she replied.

'OJ! Do you hear that? That is too cute,' Charlie teased.

Gina could have kicked herself, she really could. Or at least, she could have kicked him.

'It's cooooold,' Min complained.

Although she had been going to school in Scotland for four years now, she still wasn't used to the cold here. It was never, ever this freezing in South Africa! There, you wouldn't think twice about stepping out for the evening in a flimsy dress and nice shoes, but here? Brrrrr . . . She pulled her jacket around her tightly and tried not to let her teeth chatter.

Then, in the distance, she saw two boys coming

along the pavement towards them. They were both wearing long coats and seemed to be chatting to each other.

Min looked closely, but they were still too far away and it was too dark for her to see if one of them was Greg.

One of the boys waved, and he and his friend started jogging towards them.

'Hi!' he called out, and Min recognized him as Dermot.

'Hi!' she replied.

As they passed under a streetlamp, she saw that he was with Greg.

'I found him wandering helplessly, so I befriended him,' Dermot teased. 'Where's Gina?'

'Already gone in with Amy. The advance party,' Min told him, hyper-aware of Greg, but not daring to look at him yet.

'I was not wandering helplessly,' Greg insisted.

Min's eyes found Greg's. 'Hi,' she repeated with a generous smile, just for him.

'Hello there – are we all brave enough to go in then?' he asked.

'Course,' Niffy answered casually, and pressed the bell. 'Finn's sister and co.,' she barked into the intercom.

'What's up with her?' Dermot whispered to Min.

'Big storm brewing – you know . . .' Min checked that Niffy was ahead of them and out of earshot before whispering back, 'The Amy-Niffy-Finn love-triangle.'

'Ah,' Dermot said – he'd obviously heard something about it from Gina.

As Min climbed the stairs, she couldn't help noticing that Greg was a few paces behind her – no chance of exchanging a word, or even brushing against him.

They'd smiled hello. Smiled! Not even a handshake! At least if they'd shaken hands they would have touched. Was there ever going to be any kissing? How did you even go about getting it started? Maybe, like Niffy had said, if it didn't happen on date one, it just wasn't going to happen.

Charlie Fotheringham was at the door of the flat, playing the host. He boomed a hello, and then leered at them. 'Min, I remember you – you're looking very foxy . . . Niffy, of course . . . mwah, mwah.' She was kissed on both cheeks. Greg and Dermot were acknowledged – Greg with a nod; Dermot with raised eyebrows and obvious disapproval.

Dermot and Charlie had come across each other in the café before – with unhappy results.

'Oh yes, you're the *waiter* who dates the Yank,' Charlie said snootily.

'Something like that,' Dermot managed, muttering, 'And you're the prat who winds everyone up,' so only Niffy and Greg could hear.

'What?' Charlie demanded, suspecting he'd been insulted.

'Nothing, your lordship,' Dermot replied innocently.

'Well, in you come – we'll not ask you to fetch our drinks, just this once.'

'You are too kind.' Dermot forced himself to button his lip and not add any further insults. He would quite like to smack Charlie some time, he thought, but he didn't exactly want to start a fight in this chi-chi little hallway.

Jeez! Look at this place. This was half a million pounds worth of prime Georgian property – and it was somebody's student flat!

'Dermot!'

Dermot's mind was taken off the stunning injustices of the world by the sight of Gina, in the kitchen doorway, glowingly pretty in a perfect cream-coloured dress. He had to look her over approvingly before moving in for a hello kiss.

'You look great. I love your boots,' he told her.

'Ooooh, the boots – all I ever hear is how everybody loves the boots,' she said with a smile.

'We do. We also love the tasty tanned legs inside them.'

'You are too cute,' she told him. 'Way too cute.'

And he was too, in his blue denim shirt and rumpled chinos . . . his startlingly blue eyes fixed on hers . . . and, best of all, his ready smile. He was always smiling, teasing or joking. That was what she liked most about him. Unlike the other boys she'd met in Scotland – from Craigiefield and St Lennox – Dermot never took himself too seriously.

'Let's skip out of here and go somewhere else together,' Dermot said against her ear, his lip brushing the bottom of her earlobe and making the hairs on her neck stand up.

'I can't – not right now,' she replied. 'I need to keep an eye on Niffy. I'm worried that she and Amy might have a big fight and I want to try and stop them having some hideous scene they're going to totally regret – in fact' – Gina shrugged herself out of Dermot's arms – 'where is Niff? Has she gone into the sitting room?'

Gina went in and looked around, trying to establish what was going on.

Finn and Amy were entangled on a small white sofa

– that was pretty obvious. Everyone else in the room was doing their best to ignore them. Min and Greg were sitting on another small sofa talking to each other, their chins both very seriously propped up on their hands.

As both sofas were occupied, the rest of the guests were standing around chatting, holding glasses of wine or juice or cans of beer.

Then Gina saw Niffy. At first glance it looked as if she was talking to Charlie as she sipped at a large glass of red wine. But really, Gina saw, she wasn't paying the slightest attention to him; she was just standing beside him, nodding as if she was listening. All her focus was on her brother and his new girlfriend and their incredible enthusiasm for each other, which was on plain view for all to see.

'Hi, Niffy.' Gina decided to go over and try and distract her. She had Dermot's hand in hers and pulled him along too, although a cosy chat with Charlie was just about the last thing on his mind.

Niffy turned and gave a sour little smile. 'Finn hasn't looked at me once!' she said in disbelief. 'He can't unstick his lips from Amy's face for long enough to even say hello. To me! His one and only bloody sibling.' She brought the wine glass up to her lips and took a recklessly large gulp.

'So you brought your little waiter friend along?'
Charlie said to Gina.

'Yeah . . . get over it,' she snapped straight back at
him.

Dermot had the sense to stand back and say
nothing, although he could feel his fingernails squeeze
into his palms. If this guy did anything rude or stupid
– or even slightly irritating – Dermot would hit him.
He really would.

Gina moved so that she was blocking Niffy's view of
the Amy-and-Finn snogathon. 'So' – she racked her
brain for some topic of conversation, however bizarre
– 'it looks like Greg and Min are getting on really
well.'

'Not as well as some people,' came Niffy's snarled
reply.

Gina elbowed Dermot in the ribs, hoping to spur
him into action. Surely if anyone could make a joke of
this and take Niffy's mind off it, it had to be him.

'Has anyone seen any snacks?' Dermot asked. 'I
know you like a good snack, Niffy, and to be honest
I'm quite partial to a little cheesy cocktail nibble
myself. What I'd really like to see' – he scanned the
room – 'is a big plate of nachos – but you know, I'd
settle for a handful of peanuts . . . or even a Twiglet in
a snack emergency. But it's not much of a snack, is it,

really, a Twiglet? I mean, *Marmite*? Who in their right mind likes Marmite?'

'I bloody well do,' came Charlie's response, and he squared himself up to Dermot, as if preparing to actually fight for the right to like Marmite.

'Ah well,' Dermot began, 'I did say who in their right—'

Gina knew what was coming.

Holy cow!

There was going to be a fight! But not the Niffy and Amy one she'd expected: Dermot and Charlie were going to have a punch-up right here in the middle of Max's sister's gorgeous little Parisian-chic sitting room.

'Finn!' she squeaked in desperation in the direction of the sofa and the snogathon. 'Hi! How are you? Come and talk to us. Charlie wants a word.'

Without even turning his head, Finn continued to tickle Amy's tonsils with his tongue – or whatever it was he was doing down there – but he did hold out his hand and show two fingers. Maybe that was meant to say *Just give me two seconds*, or maybe two minutes . . . or two hours.

Whatever was meant, it had an inflammatory effect on Niffy. She screamed – she actually let out a blood-curdling shriek – then stepped towards Finn and Amy and launched her entire glass of wine at them.

Except that Gina had jumped forward to try and stop her.

For a split second, an arc of red wine just seemed to hang there in mid-air before it splattered at high velocity right over the entire front of Gina's beautiful cream dress. Any droplets not immediately soaked up by the soft pale wool landed on the white sofa and the caramel sisal below, where they were instantly sucked up, never, ever to be removed.

'Not in my right mind, eh?' Charlie growled, and punched Dermot hard on the cheek.

Stunned though he undoubtedly was, Dermot didn't have the slightest hesitation in balling up his fist and punching Charlie straight back.

Before Gina could even gasp in horror at her utterly ruined dress, she was gasping at the sight of Charlie and Dermot wrestling with one another in the middle of the room.

'Boys! Boys!' Max tried to intervene. 'Not in here! Calm down. Cut it out right now. This has to stop! Right. Now!'

Another boy got up and helped to pull the pair apart. They stood glaring at each other, both rubbing at the bruises springing up on their faces.

'Gina!' Min was the first to rush over to her friend's side. 'Gina, your beautiful dress.'

'White wine,' Niffy instructed. 'If you spill red wine over something, you need to chuck white wine straight over it. Has anyone got some?'

'Not even "sorry"!' Gina stormed at Niffy. 'You're not even going to apologize before you start throwing something else at me?'

Niffy had the decency to look slightly sheepish. 'Erm . . . I'm sorry.'

Finn and Amy had finally stopped snogging, and Amy stood up to help assess the dress damage. Her chin, Niffy noticed, looked very red – scraped and scratched by Finn's stubble – and her lips were puffy. Her dress strap had fallen down over one shoulder and her carefully combed and straightened hair was all over the place.

'Hi, Lou,' Finn said – but he didn't get up: he knew he would need to calm down quite a lot before he risked doing that.

However, Niffy didn't understand this – she thought he was adding insult to injury by not coming over to give her a hug and a kiss. She didn't reply; she just turned her attention to Gina once again.

'Salt?' Min was suggesting. 'Salt absorbs wine . . . If you take the dress off, we could try covering it in salt.'

'No!' Gina protested. 'I don't want anyone to put

anything else on it.' She sounded almost as upset as she felt.

'What about if we rinse it out in cold water?' Amy asked. 'That shouldn't do it any harm, and it would be better than letting the wine dry.'

'Noooo!' Gina wailed in protest, a wave of distress washing over her. 'What will I wear? I can't sit here in a soaking wet dress. I want to go back to the boarding house.'

That was when everyone realized they couldn't go anywhere – and they would have to do something about Gina's dress because otherwise they were going to be caught out. They couldn't go back early because that would suggest they weren't at a dinner party at Willow's house, and if they were having dinner at Willow's house and Gina had been covered in red wine, Willow would have lent her a new outfit.

'We can't go back yet,' Amy said firmly. 'We'd have far too much explaining to do to the Neb. She might even take it upon herself to phone Willow's mother and ask why we were given red wine anyway.'

'Oh no . . . I don't want to stay here,' Gina wailed.

Dermot came to stand beside her. 'Well, that makes two of us then. Shall we go? Find a bite to eat? Hook up with these guys later? I'm sure if you button your coat up over that *tiny* little spill there, it won't show too much. Or just say it's the fashion . . . new Jackson Pollock splatter style.' He tried to jolly Gina along, but she wasn't smiling.

'I think you should go,' Charlie called over to Dermot from the far side of the room.

'Delighted,' Dermot replied, and gave a low and mocking bow. He took Gina by the hand, and together they retrieved her coat and bag; then, full of relief, they headed out of the flat.

At which point Niffy walked straight up to her brother and said, 'You can't trust her. I've found out that she's still seeing Jason.'

Chapter Twenty-seven

'Lovely friends, lovely party – you must invite me again,' Dermot teased as he and Gina sat down at a tiny wooden table in the cute diner he'd steered her towards.

'Those boys aren't my friends, you know that,' Gina protested immediately. 'And anyway, I've never met any of your friends – maybe they're much worse.'

Dermot picked up the menu and studied it closely. Then, peeping over the top, he said, 'Maybe I haven't got any.'

'Don't joke!' Gina told him off. 'I should meet your friends. I bet they're dying to meet me, or . . .' She paused. 'Have you not told them anything about your Californian . . . *girlfriend*?' She said the word as quickly and as lightly as she could, because it still felt new and slightly risky.

'No, no,' Dermot said, reaching across the table to hold her hand. 'Not told them one thing about my gorgeous, tanned, blonde Californian girlfriend. Not a word . . . Of course I have!' he added when he saw the worried look on her face. 'Don't be getting all jealous on me again. There is no Scarlett, remember – except in your head . . . and on the St Jude's stage of course. Why do I not have a ticket to that yet?'

The thought of Dermot coming to St Jude's and actually watching the play was so embarrassing that Gina blushed from her neck right up to the roots of her hair.

'Whoa!' Dermot told her, and began to fan her hot cheeks with his hand.

'It's not a school play, open to parents and friends,' Gina explained. 'It's just a house drama competition. So only pupils get to watch.'

'Shame!'

'No . . . not really.' Gina shook her head and giggled a little, now that the blush was dying down.

'What would I have found out about you and me? I wonder,' Dermot asked, his face once again hidden by the menu. Putting on a high, girlie voice, he added, '*She's crazy about you, Dermot, totally crazy—*'

'Shut up!' Gina ordered. 'You might have found out how mad I was with you – how close I came to never, ever returning your calls.'

'OK . . . time to turn our attention to the menu –

all that fighting gives a boy an appetite, you know.'

'How's your face?' she asked. In reply, Dermot lowered the menu and turned his tender jaw towards her.

She gave it a gentle rub. 'Owwww,' she sympathized. 'Things often seem to get dangerous when we meet up.'

'Yeah . . . be careful what you order.'

'How about chocolate milkshakes and the home-made quarter-pounder with chips to share?'

In the taxi on the way back to the boarding house, the mood was tense and angry.

'Just keep your coat buttoned up and don't let the Neb see anything,' Amy instructed. 'If she does see the spill, it happened right at the end of the party when Willow's dad let his glass slip. OK? Everyone clear on that?'

All she got in response to this were some mutters. Although sharing a hamburger and a brownie with Dermot had gone some way to easing the pain, Gina was still really upset about her dress.

Min had spent most of her evening trying to keep Niffy and Amy apart; she hadn't had another chance to talk to Greg at length. Then he'd left half an hour before her with yet another handshake-only goodbye.

They were doomed. The whole thing was a disaster. And she liked him so much!

Niffy and Amy were at opposite sides of the taxi, still furious with each other. The seething had continued all evening.

Amy rubbed her forehead. She'd only drunk half a glass of wine but she had a raging headache and she felt exhausted. What on earth was the matter with Niffy?! It was as if she'd gone mad. After Niffy's outburst about Jason, Amy had looked at Finn in astonishment, but he had just laughed it off.

'Lou! Calm down,' he'd told her. 'I think I can see for myself that Amy's happy to be here with me, and that's all I care about.'

For the rest of the evening Amy had kept as close to Finn as she could, not wanting Niffy to come and spread any more lies about her.

Niffy had aimed that glass of wine at her! At her lovely new dress. The girl was just plain vindictive. And the Jason outburst – that was just horrible. Horrible!

Suddenly Amy found herself thinking about toast: white toast, absolutely dripping with butter. Smeared with layer after layer of butter, just the way her gran used to make it for her when she was little. Oh! She couldn't stop thinking about toast. The smell of toast, the warm melted butter . . . She almost had to move her jaws, the sensation of eating toast was so real. But there wasn't going to be any toast-eating, she told herself sternly. She tried to focus on willowy Peta. Then she looked down and thought about her own now very small waist, tightly encircled by the sparkly dress.

The taxi braked and drew up outside the boarding house.

'Just play it cool,' Amy reminded them as they walked towards the front door. It was two minutes to eleven, so even the Neb, who kept her eyes fixed firmly to the clock at this time of night, couldn't accuse them of being late.

After an evening out, the boarding-house girls had to sign themselves back in again, so they headed for Mrs Knebworth's sitting room, where they found her surrounded by some of the younger girls, who were watching a film on the TV.

'Oh, hello,' she called out cheerily as she saw Min and Niffy coming into the room. 'Had a good evening, have you?'

'Yes,' Min answered.

'Delicious food,' Gina said, just ducking her head round the door. Her coat was buttoned right up to the top but she was worried that the Neb might smell the wine – and sniff out the crimes they had committed this evening.

'It was Willow McIver's house you were visiting tonight, wasn't it?' the housemistress asked. 'Julia . . .?' She looked around the little group of girls and found the face she wanted. 'Weren't you saying you'd been there a few times, because you know Willow's younger sister?'

Min, Niffy and Gina's expressions stiffened. Julia had been to Willow's house before – several times! This was a disaster. Now, absolutely no doubt about it, the Neb was going to ask them some complicated question about the house and they were going to be in deepest do-do.

'I'm not feeling so great . . .' Amy was standing behind the other three girls clutching her head, which was getting worse and worse.

Gina turned just in time to see two surprising things: the colour draining completely from Amy's face, and a look of shock crossing Niffy's face as she saw this happen.

'Amy!' Gina cried.

Niffy was closest and caught hold of Amy as she wobbled. Gina rushed over and managed to grab her before she crumpled to the floor.

'Oh dear, oh dear!' Mrs Knebworth exclaimed, and

got to her feet. 'Put her in this chair,' she instructed. 'Head down between her knees.'

Once she was sitting down Amy let out a little groan.

'How are you doing?' Mrs Knebworth asked.

'Better,' Amy insisted, wanting to avoid any more fuss and get out of the room as soon as possible.

'Didn't you eat much at Willow's?' the Neb wanted to know. 'People usually faint when they've not had enough to eat – or they've been drinking,' she added suspiciously.

'I think I'm just a bit tired,' Amy replied, running her hands over her pale, sweaty face.

'OK, well, we'll let Luella and Gina here help you up to bed – but any more fainting or feeling sick or anything and I want to know straight away. Did you eat anything unusual?' the Neb added.

'No, not at all,' Gina insisted.

'Roast beef with all the trimmings,' Niffy remembered to say.

'And the McIvers obviously gave you nothing to drink?' was Mrs Knebworth's next question.

'No,' Gina, Niffy and Amy all said together.

First Gina and then a reluctant Niffy put an arm round Amy's waist and began helping her up to the dorm.

There was silence between the three at first – Amy and Niffy still determined not to acknowledge one another, and Gina racking her brain for the right thing to say.

'You looked worried when Amy fainted,' Gina blurted out.

'Yeah?' Niffy said, sounding surprised.

'Yeah.'

'Impossible.'

'So you actually want me to be ill?' Amy piped up all of a sudden between them.

Niffy shrugged.

Amy stopped and let her arms drop so that she was no longer being supported. Then she turned to Niffy and suddenly aimed a punch at her.

Niffy saw it coming and swivelled to the side.

Despite the headache, despite the dizziness, despite her raging hunger, Amy still managed to shout at her, 'What is your problem? Just what exactly is your problem?!'

'Jason!' Niffy replied furiously.

'What has Jason got to do with anything?' Amy demanded.

'I met him on the bus. On Thursday.' Niffy said it as if it would explain everything.

'So what?' Amy asked, although she felt slightly

startled by this chance meeting. She'd thought so little about Jason lately, she was almost surprised to hear that he was still around, still taking buses, still chatting to girls.

'He told me,' Niffy said, thinking this would make it clear to Amy.

'Told you what? I have *no idea* what you're talking about!'

It was at this point that Niffy began to have her first doubts. Amy looked so angry and so astonished. She also looked so pale and just terrible – maybe Niffy had somehow got it wrong.

With less venom in her voice now, she said, 'He told me you've been emailing him every week – asking to meet up . . . and that you're seeing him tomorrow.'

Amy's furious glare fell from her face, and instead she just gave Niffy a pitying look. 'And I suppose you believed every word the lying cheat said to you.' Without another word, she headed off down the corridor.

After drinking a glass of water, Amy took off her dress, hung it up carefully and got into bed.

With a series of stomps, crashing of doors and banging of drawers, Niffy undressed, stuffed her clothes away and went to bed too.

Gina headed into the bathroom, where she ran a

sinkful of cold water and then gingerly lowered in her stained dress.

Min, wrapped in her dressing gown, came in after her.

'Did you have fun?' Gina asked her friend.

'Yeah,' Min said with a half-hearted shrug. 'Well . . . with Greg, yes – but everything else is a disaster.'

Gina nodded. 'I know.'

'Gina?' Min began as she loaded up her toothbrush with toothpaste. 'I don't think Amy's eaten anything all day.'

'I know,' Gina agreed. 'She told us she'd stop this, but she hasn't.'

It was nearly one a.m. when Gina, lying restlessly awake, had the idea.

She slipped out of bed, put her feet into her ballet slippers, found her dressing gown on the back of the door and tiptoed out of the dorm.

The boarding house was always creepy at night. The only light was the orangey glow of the nightlights in the stairwell. It was strange to be amongst so many people and yet surrounded by silence and stillness.

As quietly as she could, she slipped along the shadowy downstairs corridor until she came to the Upper Fifth sitting room.

Gently, gently, she turned the handle and opened the door. It creaked noisily on its hinges. Stepping into the room, Gina listened for a long time, but couldn't hear anyone stirring.

She went over to the computer, turned it on and waited for it to go through its whirring – then finally she called up the Internet page and logged on to her account.

The corner of the screen told her that it was 1.15 a.m. GMT, so in California it would be late afternoon. With any luck she would get a reply straight away.

She opened a new email page, filled in Paula, Maddison and Ria's email addresses at the top, then typed out her message:

```
Hi guys,
Missing you! I can't sleep because
I'm so worried about a friend of
mine here. Her name is Amy. P and M,
you met her, remember?
    She isn't eating. I've tried to
speak to her about it, but that
hasn't worked. Should I speak to
someone else? As you know, our
housemistress is a bit of an
```

old-fashioned DRAGON lady and
I can't think of a teacher who I
really, really trust.

    Guys, I don't know what to do.
Because of what's happened to Ria's
sister and because you're my oldest
friends, I hoped you might be able
to give me some good advice.

    I love you!

    Gina xx

Chapter Twenty-eight

After school Min walked back to the boarding house alone. Her rucksack was really heavy. One drawback to doing more S-grades than anyone else in her year was that she had to carry more books and jotters around; she also had far more homework.

She felt a bit like a snail, crawling along with this big heavy load on her back. The afternoon was cold and grey; early December winds had stripped all the remaining withered brown leaves from the trees and the grey sky promised darkness and more rain.

Back at home in Durban, her little brothers and sisters would be finishing school too. But they would be scampering home in T-shirts and sandals, preparing to go out and play in the sunny garden. Min felt a pang of homesickness and decided to phone home this evening. She and her family emailed regularly, but it would be really nice to hear their voices – although sometimes phone calls were the worst because after you'd finished talking and had to hang up, you felt so far away.

Min wanted to tell her mum about Greg, but she really wasn't sure how it would go down. And she still wasn't exactly sure what to call Greg. Was he really a boyfriend? Did someone who took you to cafés and museums, who talked to you really intensely, really enthusiastically, but never once held your hand or tried to kiss you – did he count as a boyfriend?

She didn't know. She didn't know who to ask for advice either. Amy and Niffy thought she was just being silly: 'Just give him a kiss, for goodness' sake! . . . Just lean over and kiss his cheek! . . . Give him the idea! . . . It really isn't that big a deal!' they'd insisted.

But it was. Or it seemed to be. Or it was turning into one.

Although Greg had already asked her if she wanted to meet up next weekend, Min had a feeling that this couldn't go on much longer. She had to do something; she had to give him some sort of sign or signal that she wanted things to go a little bit further. If they could just hold hands and kiss, she would relax. She wouldn't feel so tense about what was going to happen or when.

Tongues? To be honest, Min was concerned about tongues; she didn't know if she really wanted to do that. When she'd glanced surreptitiously at Amy and

Finn on Saturday night . . . well, it had looked rather messy and slobbery. But holding hands and giving little kisses on the neck like the ones she saw Dermot give Gina, now that looked . . . nice.

Maybe she would write Greg a letter. A poem! The idea made her smile. Could she write him a poem telling him how she felt? Maybe she wouldn't sign it. Maybe she would write it, post it and never mention it. Never admit it was hers – just see what happened. See if it made any difference at all.

As soon as she got back to the boarding house, Min dumped her coat in her locker and hauled her heavy bag along to the study. If she was going to try and write a poem, she would need peace, quiet, and maybe a book or two from the library for inspiration.

'Where are you off to?' Amy asked as she ran into Min in the corridor. 'The study already? Not even time for a cup of tea with us?'

'No,' Min told her. 'Hectic schedule.' She pointed at her heavy bag.

'You poor old thing,' Amy sympathized, as she carried on past in the other direction.

Min sat at her desk in the silent study room. She opened a page of her notebook and selected a nice sharp pencil. She stared at the page.

Kissing, she wrote down. Then she scored it out.

A kiss, she wrote underneath. She stared at it.

Is a very strange thing, she added.

She stared some more.

She looked out of the window. Then she chewed the end of the pencil. Good grief! This was hard. Maths problems and physics equations were much, much easier than this. They had a question and an answer. This . . . this felt like plucking something completely unknown from the air. She had no idea how to do it.

A kiss is a very strange thing, she read.

Taking hold of her pencil again, she added, *I don't know how to start it. I don't know how to end it. I don't know where to begin.*

Begin rhymed with *thing* – well, almost. That was surely a good thing. Maybe she could work with that.

All of a sudden, a look of determination came over Min's face. Her pencil hovered over the page and she suddenly felt ready to grapple with words and create something brand new.

'Pssssst, Min,' came a whisper right against her ear.

Min instinctively cupped her hand round her work, not wanting anyone to read what she'd written. She looked up to see Amy holding out a small envelope.

'You were in such a hurry to get to the study, you

didn't check the post,' Amy told her, and held out the envelope.

Min took it. It was small and white with her name on the front in careful black handwriting.

'Who's it from?' Amy asked. 'You never get letters unless they're from your mum. And this isn't air mail.'

'I don't know,' Min replied, puzzled.

'C'mon, open it,' Amy instructed. Clearly she was going to stay right here until she found out what was inside the envelope too.

Min tore open the flap and brought out a small, folded piece of cream-coloured paper. She opened it up and saw, written in the same careful black hand-writing . . . a poem!

'What is it?' Amy asked, desperate to know.

'It's a note – I think it's from Greg,' she stumbled, because who else could it be from? 'And it's private,' she added, and folded the paper up again.

'Oh! OK then!' Amy rolled her eyes and reluctantly took several steps away from Min's desk.

Now Min carefully laid the piece of paper down on her desk. She opened it, she smoothed it out and very slowly she read the words Greg had written:

When I close my eyes
I dream of kissing you.
But when I open them again
I don't know if I dare.
Your eyes say yes, but
How much do you care?
When I close my eyes
I dream of kissing you.

It was a little cheesy – it was kind of embarrassing and corny . . . but . . . but Min couldn't help herself. She folded the paper up into a tiny, tiny square and tucked it into her pencil case. She couldn't wipe the astonished smile off her face as she wondered what her mum would think.

'Sorry to interrupt your happy thoughts . . .' Amy began.

'Oh!' Min was snapped back to the study room.

'I was just wondering – if I gave you Jason's email address . . . would you consider . . . ?'

'Writing to him and telling him to explain himself? With pleasure,' Min said. 'Do you think it will help?'

Amy sighed, then answered: 'Finn and I don't have a hope if Niffy and I can't get over this.'

Chapter Twenty-nine

'*Gina! Phone!*'

Gina heard the shout in the corridor, dropped what she was doing and hurried out of the dorm. She rushed down to the little payphone housed in a booth under the stairs.

Dermot? she wondered. Or her family? Menzie? She hadn't spoken to her little brother for ages! These were the only possibilities. No one else ever phoned her on the boarding-house landline. It was so hard to get through for a start.

'Hi,' she said, as soon as she picked up the receiver.

'*Hi!*' a chorus of voices came back at her.

'Paula? Maddison?' Gina asked.

'And me!' came Ria's voice. 'We're on speaker phone. This is a conference call,' she joked.

'How are you guys?' Gina asked.

'We're fine but you need help,' Paula replied.

'I know,' Gina agreed, delighted that they'd

responded to her email so quickly. 'How's your sister, Ria?' she wanted to know.

'She's doing well, but she's still in hospital. It's going to take a really long time for her to get better. It's so awful,' Ria told her, 'but I think it's also kind of embarrassing. She was beautiful and healthy and she made *herself* so sick, she nearly died. She could still die.'

'Oh, Ria,' Gina said quietly. 'I had no idea how bad it was.'

'No . . . we didn't either,' Maddison added.

'So you have totally got to help your friend,' Ria went on, 'before it gets anything like as bad as it was with Megan.'

Gina gripped the receiver tightly. They were scaring her. How could she help Amy? Why was it down to her?

'What should I do?' she asked her friends nervously.

'We're going to send you as much help as we can,' Paula told her calmly. 'We'll email you loads of website addresses and links, for on-line advice you can give to Amy. Ria's put a self-help book in the post and we've even looked up British helpline numbers. But you're the one who's going to have to give all this to Amy.'

'Just do it gently and kindly,' Maddison suggested. 'Tell her that other people know how she feels – there is plenty of help out there; she just needs to go find it. She just needs to ask. No one else even needs to know apart from the people she really trusts.'

'Oh . . . this is too scary,' Gina admitted. 'What if I get it all wrong? What if I make everything much worse? She could get really, really sick, like your sister, Ria.'

'No one noticed what was going on with Megan,' Maddison said. 'Maybe if someone had seen it earlier, it wouldn't have got so bad.'

Gina stared at the blue walls of the phone booth. She wanted to stay in here. She didn't want to go upstairs and do this really difficult thing: confront her friend about her problem again. It hadn't worked the first time – plus she and Min still hadn't been able to get Amy and Niffy back together again. If she couldn't even help them to do that, how on earth could she help Amy face the fact that she no longer knew how to eat normally?

'Guys,' Gina began, 'I don't know if I can do this.'

'You can!' Paula insisted. 'We'll help you. You can call us, you can email us – you can even get Amy to speak to us if you think that will help.'

'Thank you,' Gina said, and felt a lump in her throat. Her friends were so far away, but all three of them were also right here. She could hear them talking and breathing, sounding so close; willing her to do OK, wanting to help out in any way they could.

'Cool books, leaflets and anything else we could think of are in the post,' Maddison assured her.

'They'll take a few days,' Ria added. 'Until then, you need to talk to Amy and maybe get her to check out the websites we've emailed you.'

'Right . . . OK,' Gina heard herself agree, although she still didn't know how she was going to do this.

'This is serious, Gina,' Ria told her. 'You *have* to help her!'

Chapter Thirty

On Thursday morning Gina watched Amy eating her breakfast of two small oatcakes with a scrape of honey and no butter.

For several days now, she had been watching her friend and noticing all sorts of things – but she still hadn't summoned up the courage to talk to her about the problem.

Gina had spent three whole lunch breaks waiting for Amy to show up in the dining room – to no avail. Plus, she noted that Amy would come back from school, drink two glasses of water and lie down for the hour and a half before supper.

At supper, Gina saw how slowly Amy ate her small main course and tiny helping of pudding. Sometimes she had to marvel at her friend's amazing restraint. But mainly she just felt sorry for her.

Amy looked so pale and tired now. She'd become moody and sulky. She didn't talk much in the evenings

– she fretted about her performance in the play and went over her lines anxiously. She didn't turn up at hockey lessons any more. She went to the library, instructing Gina to tell the teacher that she had a bad stomach.

Gina wasn't sure what it was about hockey practice that Amy disliked most: the fact that Niffy now played on Penny's team, or the fact that she'd eaten so little, she didn't have the energy to run around.

It was clear that Amy was conserving energy. She kept quiet in class. She walked slowly. She saved up all her strength to come alive on stage during her lunch time and evening rehearsals.

Today, Gina went to the rehearsal after school and watched in awe as the words she'd so carefully crafted came to life on stage. Amy, Peta and Jamie were really good, really convincing. Gina watched them with an amazed tingle: her words were suddenly real – and the biggest change was in Amy. When she was up there on the stage, with the bright lights illuminating her blonde hair and white skin, she glowed just like her old self again.

But as soon as the rehearsal was over, she seemed to shrink and collapse again. She shuffled back to the boarding house, hugging her coat around her, totally spent by her performance.

Walking back from the rehearsal with her, Gina had almost found the courage to say the words: 'Amy, you're not eating enough – you've got to talk to me about it.'

But at the last moment she'd chickened out.

All the next day, Friday, in every single class, Gina watched as Amy sat listless and quiet, and told herself that today was going to be the day. She promised herself that she would not go to bed tonight without having the conversation.

She'd followed the links herself now; she'd been on the websites and she'd read much of the advice. Amy had to face up to what was going on. She was getting dangerously thin: her body was no longer being properly fed; soon her mind was going to be affected too. Then it would be much, much harder to bring her round.

The last lesson of the day was history. The class-room was hot, the lesson dull, but even so, Amy was looking unusually exhausted. She held her head in her hands as if her neck didn't have the strength to support it by itself.

Somehow, Gina lost Amy in the locker rooms. She looked around, planning to walk back to the boarding house with her, but then Amy had disappeared.

Gina hurried out of the school building, hoping to spot her friend. As she emerged, she saw Amy's blonde head through the railings. She was heading off in the opposite direction to the boarding house.

Without giving it much thought, Gina buttoned up her coat and began to follow her. Boarding-house girls weren't allowed out of the school grounds without the express permission of the Neb, but this afternoon Gina would have to ignore that rule. This was an emergency. If she had to, she would explain it all later.

Amy was walking quickly. Her collar was turned up and her head was down, as if she didn't want anyone to see her.

Gina kept a safe distance away, but she had Amy well in her sights. She was hurrying down the side streets towards the busy main road that passed close to the school.

As she rounded the corner, Gina saw Amy turn into the mini-supermarket. Now she wasn't sure what to do. Cross the road and watch to see when Amy came out? Follow her into the shop?

Gina decided to cross the road. She picked a doorway with a deep recess and stood there, hoping she would be able to see Amy without being spotted herself.

Several long minutes passed. Gina stared at the

entrance of the shop, hoping she'd not somehow missed her friend coming out. She glanced at her watch. Hopefully, in all the bustle of Friday afternoon at the boarding house, she and Amy wouldn't be missed. But if they were . . . A weekend of being gated loomed.

There was Amy! She was coming out of the shop with a huge, bulging carrier bag in her hand.

Keeping a safe distance, Gina followed her friend back towards the school again. Once Amy had passed through the gates, Gina let the distance between them widen. She was almost certain Amy was heading back to the boarding house now, so there was no need to follow her so closely.

Gina came in through the front door, prepared to tell the Neb that she'd had to stay behind and help tidy up the biology lab after a spill, but she wasn't questioned. A group of Year Fours was packing up for a Duke of Edinburgh hiking trip, which was monopolizing all Mrs Knebworth's attention.

Gina unloaded her coat and bags, then went straight up to the dorm, expecting to find Amy and her mysterious bag of groceries.

But there was just Min in the dorm; she was smiling a welcome.

She couldn't wait to tell Gina her news. 'My mum is

really pleased for me! She says Greg sounds lovely and she'll ask the Neb for permission for me to go out to the cinema with him. An evening date! Maybe if she emails it, we could even go out tomorrow night!'

Gina smiled too. She was happy for her friend, but she had Amy and the bulging bag of groceries on her mind.

'That's great . . . but have you seen Amy?'

Min shook her head.

'I need to find her,' Gina said, and hurried out of the dorm.

She ran into Niffy, but when she asked her if she'd seen Amy, she met with an indifferent shrug of the shoulders.

Gina went in search of Rosie, but when she found her in the Year Four sitting room, she didn't have any news about Amy either.

Gina tried the study, the bathrooms, the laundry room – even Mel's room. There was no trace of Amy.

There was nowhere else left in the boarding house. Where had Amy and her large bag of shopping gone?!

Gina felt anxious. She felt responsible. She should have told someone else what she'd seen. Maybe she was out of her depth here. Maybe she should call on an adult to help . . .

As she walked along the ground-floor corridor,

planning to go back upstairs to her dorm and confide in Min and Niffy, she happened to glance down the small passage that led to the visitors' toilet.

There was a small gap under the toilet door and Gina thought she saw a flash of bright orange. The same orange as the mini-market carrier bag!

Taking several very quiet steps down the corridor, Gina bent down to take a closer look. Yes, there was no doubt in her mind now. That was definitely the same bag.

Gina had spent enough time on the eating disorder websites to understand immediately what was going on. Amy had locked herself in the visitors' toilet with a bag full of food. She was going to binge and maybe even make herself sick afterwards.

Gina wanted to bang on the door. She wanted to shout for help. She felt sweaty with fear for her friend . . . but she remained frozen to the spot, with no idea what to do.

Chapter Thirty-one

Amy sat on the toilet seat lid and looked around the little room. It was neat and white and smelled of the rose-scented pot pourri that Mrs Knebworth had placed on the small windowsill. It was a very old-fashioned bathroom – the only one in the Victorian boarding house that hadn't been updated with modern fittings. The toilet seat was pale wood, bleached almost white with decades of scrubbing and cleaning. The enamel of the porcelain basin on the wall was decorated with a web of faint grey cracks, and the chunky silver taps had old HOT and COLD labels enamelled on top.

It was peaceful here; one of the quietest, most private places in the whole house. Amy was grateful to be in here, safely locked behind the thick brass bolt which she'd pulled firmly shut. Even if someone hammered on that door for her to come out, she wouldn't. She was safe here.

She held her head in her hands, realizing how tired she was. But she had managed it. She had gone from Monday through to Friday without eating a single full-sized meal, and missing lunch every day. All through the week she had promised herself a reward. A really big treat for such good behaviour.

She had thought all week about what the treat would be: a chocolate bar, a packet of salt and vinegar crisps, a thickly buttered slice of white bread, or a Kit Kat, her favourite biscuit. All week she had thought about food. That was the problem when you didn't eat much: you *obsessed* about it. You thought about it, imagined it, even dreamed about wonderful buffet spreads.

She had meant to go to the mini-market and choose just one or two treats, but somehow when she was in the shop, she couldn't choose, couldn't decide, seemed to lose all control, and had found herself stuffing her basket absolutely full of things she hadn't even thought about since she was a little girl: Tunnock's tea-cakes, chocolate digestives, Eccles cakes, fruit loaf, smooth white bread . . . She hadn't been able to stop herself.

Only the thought that she might not have enough money to pay for it all had finally brought the spree to an end.

Then she'd carried this great bulging bag of goodies back to the boarding house without much of an idea what she was going to do with it.

That's when she'd thought of locking herself in the toilet and thinking. Peace and quiet. She needed peace and quiet to try and make some sense of the jumble in her mind.

She wanted to be thin. Just like Peta. No. Thinner than Peta. She wanted to be the thinnest person on the stage, the thinnest girl in the year. If she couldn't be the prettiest or the best actress, then at least she could be the thinnest. That was under her control.

She wanted the feeling of fury with Niffy to go away. Amy had somehow linked ridding herself of fury with ridding herself of weight. As if somehow she could purge the two from her body.

Looking at the grocery bag, she felt absolutely desperate for something to eat. But she didn't want to eat. She'd worked so hard at it all week. She'd been so strong and she'd resisted so much. Now, all her efforts might be wasted. She might start on one thing in that bag and not be able to stop.

She knew that some dieters made themselves sick, but she didn't know if she wanted to do that. It was ... well, she hated being sick. It was horrible, disgusting.

Slowly she opened up the bag and looked inside. Her hand was on the packet of Tunnock's teacakes. Her gran's favourites. Almost every day her gran had one of these super-sweet chocolate-coated mallow cake things for elevenses, along with her cup of super-sugared tea. When Amy was little, she had loved these teacakes, but as she grew older, she'd found them too sweet, and now it was years since she'd eaten one.

Her hand ripped open the plastic packaging and her trembling fingers tore into the silver wrapping. She stuffed one whole teacake into her mouth, bit down on it and swallowed.

Oh! It was delicious! It was absolutely delicious – it was the best thing she'd ever, ever tasted!

She opened another one and crammed that in too. Now she spotted the white loaf of bread. She pulled open the packet and ripped a slice in half, cramming it into her mouth on top of the teacake.

Mmm! Mmmmm! She could barely chew fast enough. This was so good, so scrumptious . . . heavenly. Another piece of bread quickly followed.

She had never, ever felt so ravenously hungry before. Her body was absolutely starved! It craved food. It craved great greedy mouthfuls of everything in the bag. She couldn't open the packets quickly enough to answer the screaming *Feed me!* inside her head.

But then she thought of her gran . . . Oh, what would her gran think of her now? Starving herself all week, then ramming food into her gob like this. Her gran would be absolutely horrified!

Her gran, who had always scraped to give her family enough. Her gran, who never, ever let you leave even a mouthful on your plate because it was a waste; who saved every butter wrapper in a compartment in the fridge to grease the baking tins.

Amy was greedy.

She was wasting food.

She was going to be huge, fat, hideous.

But she couldn't stop now.

Her body was screaming like a ravenous, starving baby for food.

It was out of control.

But she had to feed it.

With both hands she stuffed a slice of bread and two digestive biscuits into her mouth, feeling hot, helpless tears of hatred roll down her face.

She didn't want to be sick. She didn't want to make herself sick. She'd never done it before – it must be horrible.

But she couldn't have all this food in her stomach.

DRAMA GIRL

Help me! Please, someone . . . Please – please help me!
These were the words roaring in her head now. But
all that came out through the crammed mouthful of
food was a stifled, muffled sob.

Chapter Thirty-two

Gina turned and ran.

She'd heard the wrappers being torn open, she'd heard the sounds of eating, chewing, more eating . . . Then she'd heard the sob.

Just the one, pained and heart-rending – then silence, as if Amy had managed to stifle everything else.

That single sob had frightened Gina more than anything else she'd seen or heard so far.

Now she knew she had to go and get help, so she ran back to her dorm.

Min was in the room with a scatter of outfits across her bed: she was obviously trying to decide what to wear for her cinema date. She looked up and saw Gina's shocked and anxious expression. 'What's up?' she asked.

'It's Amy – she's in trouble,' Gina blurted out.

Just then the door opened and Niffy stood

hesitantly in the doorway. She gave the room a quick once over to make sure Amy wasn't there, and only then did she come in.

'What is it?' she asked, catching the worried expressions on both Min and Gina's faces.

'It's Amy,' Gina said, and when Niffy just shrugged at this, she went on, 'She's in real trouble.'

'What do you mean?' Min asked.

'You know how she's not been eating properly and it's been going on for weeks now? Well, she's downstairs, locked in the visitors' toilet with this great big bag of food – and I think she's stuffing herself and maybe planning to make herself sick or something. But she's crying' – Gina heard the crack in her voice, but she stumbled on – 'and she's so upset and unhappy and . . . Guys!' She appealed to them both. 'I don't know what we're supposed to do about it, but I know that she needs us to help her!'

'Fine . . . go ahead,' Niffy said.

'What about you?' Gina asked. 'Don't you think you should come too? Don't you think maybe some of Amy's unhappiness might have something to do with you?'

Niffy shrugged again, but she had the decency to blush. 'I don't think Amy will want me there,' she added in a voice that sounded small and a little unsure.

'I have something that might help you decide,' Min said, and went over to her chest of drawers. 'I just got this, and I printed it out for you to look at . . .' She picked up a sheet of paper and brought it over to Niffy.

It took Niffy several minutes to register that she was looking at a printout of an email exchange between Jason and Min. The words: *Yes, OK, I was fibbing. I'm sorry if this has caused any problem* . . . told her everything she needed to know.

'Amy said he was lying,' Gina pointed out. 'You should have believed her.'

Niffy's shoulders seemed to sag a little.

'She really, really likes Finn,' Min added gently. 'I don't think she would hurt his feelings like that.'

'I think we should go,' Gina reminded them. 'We have to help her.'

'C'mon then,' Niffy said, and there was now a calm matter-of-factness to her voice that Gina found reassuring.

As they left the dorm, Min asked, 'What do you think we should do?'

'I'm not sure,' Gina admitted. 'But we have to tell her that we know what's happening and we want to help and we can get her help, if that's what she needs.'

'Sounds like a good plan,' Niffy agreed.

The three girls hurried down the stairs together.

'Where are you all off to?'

It was Mel: she'd just come out of her room and was standing in front of them on the landing.

Oh great! They really didn't need Mel or anyone else questioning them or getting in their way.

'Mind your own beeswax!' Niffy said, and brushed rudely past her.

'Ooooh, there's no need to be like that,' Mel replied, but she let the girls past without further interrogation.

They made it to the ground-floor corridor. But just as they were about to head down the passage to the guest loo, two sixth formers turned into the main corridor and began to walk towards them.

The friends froze, knowing they couldn't go down there now.

'Hi, Eleanor!' Niffy said cheerfully. 'So how come the first eleven lost by three goals last night?'

'No idea,' came the reply, and the two girls hurried past before they could be asked any more cheeky questions.

Now the corridor was empty, so they took their chance and went towards the locked toilet.

When they got to the door, there was an awkward silence: no one knew what to say or who should say it.

'Amy . . .?' Gina began gently. 'We know you're in there and that you're not feeling very happy.'

There was no reply, but they could hear the rustle of packaging.

'Amy' – Gina's voice sounded so kind and calm – 'you need to come out and talk to us. We all want to help you.'

When there was no response to this either, Min decided to have a go.

'Amy, whatever the problem is, we can help you. I just know we can. Think how worried I was about the whole doctor thing last term, and how you solved that for me. You worried away for me and found an answer. This is just the same, Amy,' she went on. 'We're going to help you solve the problem. Please, just give us a chance.'

Still there was only silence from the other side of the door.

Niffy leaned forward and rapped on the door firmly. 'You twinky!' she exclaimed, causing Gina and Min to gasp and poke her in the sides to try and stop her. But she carried on: 'What are you doing, Aim? You muffin-head! This is a one-way ticket to the loony bin. Is that what you want?'

'*Niffy!*' Gina stormed, grabbing her by the arm and pulling her away from the door. 'You can't say that! Just get out of here and leave this to us!'

Niffy stood rooted to the spot, looking at Gina in confusion.

Then, to their astonishment, they heard Amy's voice on the other side of the door: 'No, it's OK . . . Let her stay.'

Then they heard the sound of the bolt being pulled back.

The toilet door opened and Amy appeared before them. Her eyes looked red and swollen and her face was still streaked with traces of the tears she had tried to wipe away. She looked pale, sweaty, scared, and just terrible.

In one hand she held the horrible bulging bag of comfort food, empty wrappers spilling from the top of it.

'Oh, Amy!' Gina exclaimed, and held out her arms to give her friend a hug.

Amy leaned forward and put her head on Gina's shoulder. But as her arms went out, one took in Gina's waist and the other reached for Niffy.

'Poor Amy,' Min murmured. 'Poor old thing.' She stood behind Amy and rubbed her back comfortingly.

'Aim, I'm sorry. I'm really sorry,' Niffy said gently. 'I was wrong about Jason. I've been a total twit.' With that she put her arm round her very best friend in the whole world. The cross words of the past few weeks weren't yet forgotten, but for now they were put to one side.

'And I'm sorry I said you were squidgy,' Niffy added. 'You feel like a Twiglet.'

'H-help me,' Amy managed to stammer out finally in a choked voice. 'Please help me.'

Chapter Thirty-three

Min could feel the heat of Greg's shoulder very, very close to her own. They weren't touching but they were within touching distance. According to the laws of physics – something both Min and Greg understood very well – particles of Min's shoulder were definitely within the electro-magnetic field of Greg's. The particles were already mixing. Their atoms were already bouncing off each other, magnetically attracting one another the way Min felt magnetically attracted to Greg.

It was as if the laws of gravity were acting on her. When he was around, she couldn't help being sucked into his orbit, drawn towards him.

They were at the multiplex, in the middle of a row surrounded by the big Saturday-night audience. All around them hundreds of people were chomping their way through popcorn, nachos and chocolates and slurping at great beakers of fizz.

Greg wasn't at boarding school like Min; he was a day pupil at St Lennox, so he'd been dropped off at the cinema by his dad, carrying a small brown bag of popcorn, home made by his mum.

'How embarrassing is this?' he'd said when he met Min, holding his popcorn up in the air.

'That is so sweet!' Min had said. 'That's just the kind of thing my mum would do – you know, if she wasn't at the hospital saving babies.'

'Hey! My mum has a job too,' Greg had reminded her. 'But molecular biology professors tend to get the weekends off. Apart from marking, of course.'

He had picked the film. Now, halfway through it, Min wasn't sure she liked it. It was very boysy and action-packed, with guns and bangs, car chases and loud noises.

She kept jumping – it was embarrassing. Every time something made her jump, Greg would look at her and giggle.

In the darkness, she'd thought that maybe they would hold hands, but there was still a tantalizing ten-centimetre gap between them. Even worse, the couple in the seat beside her were holding hands, and every now and then they would stop snacking for a moment, lean towards each other and snog with loud squelching, sucking noises.

'More popcorn?' Greg whispered, holding out his brown paper bag.

'I'm fine, thanks,' Min whispered back; then, all of sudden, before she could even think about it, she turned towards Greg, leaned a little closer and asked, 'Did you send me that poem?'

There was no reply.

Greg's eyes stayed fixed on the screen in front of him, but even in the dim light Min thought she could see his cheek and then his ear actually turn pink.

'I thought it was a really sweet poem,' she added, suddenly feeling her heart hammer and a whole flock of butterflies spring up in her stomach.

When Greg still didn't turn, still didn't say anything, still didn't react, Min suddenly had a daring, falling feeling. This was it. It was now or never. She was going to have to make the first move.

It wasn't that he didn't want to; he was just too nervous, too scared. She was going to have to tell him that it was OK. Show him, even.

'Greg?' she whispered, leaning right against his ear now so that her lips were brushing his hair. 'I want to kiss you too.'

There.

She'd said it.

Min could hardly believe herself.

Super-shy, super-swotty Min. She'd just told a boy that she wanted to kiss him.

Her heart felt as if it was going to explode with fear, with fright, with breathless excitement.

Greg's head was turning.

Slowly, slowly, his face was turning towards hers.

His eyes fixed on hers and he leaned slowly, slowly towards her.

Min leaned in.

This was it, she thought.

This was finally, finally going to be it.

She let her eyelids gently close, felt her lashes brush against her cheek.

As she turned towards him, Min didn't realize that her elbow was now sweeping not just across her arm-rest but the armrest of the munching, crunching snogger beside her.

Greg's face moved so close that she could feel his breath against her cheek – and then there was an almighty explosion on the screen. Min's elbow jerked, and the snogger's tray of nachos and dip flew up into the air. Nachos scattered all over the place, followed by a light splattering of salsa sauce.

'*Hey!*' the snogger exclaimed. 'Look what you've done!'

'I'm sorry – I'm very sorry.' Min turned to apologize.

She felt almost tearfully upset. She had spoiled everything . . . again!

'Yeah, well, watch what you're doing . . .' the snogger growled. He had a chubby face, close-cropped hair, and Min felt more than a little scared of him.

'Sorry,' she repeated.

She began to brush the nachos off her lap and unfortunately put her hand into a patch of gooey tomato dip. 'Yuck!'

'Shall we go?' Greg asked in a whisper.

As Min nodded, she knew that another important moment had gone for ever.

Chapter Thirty-four

'Pass!' Amy urged Niffy urgently. 'Over here!'

Amy was racing towards the goal on long, energetic legs, hair streaming out behind her. Penny B-H was already charging towards Niffy, determined to get the ball from her, but before she could, Niffy flicked it effortlessly towards Amy.

'Nice!' She grinned as Amy stopped it, turned it and aimed it at the corner of the goal mouth with a series of deft moves.

Amy smacked the ball hard, feeling the reverberations travel up her hands. 'Goal!' she shouted. The blast of Miss McKay's whistle confirmed it.

Niffy turned to Penny B-H with a smirk on her face. 'Five–one!' she exclaimed. 'Ow-ow-ouch!'

Then she ran towards Amy and slapped her hand in a high five. 'You're coming on,' she teased her friend. 'To get as good as me, though, you'll have to eat a lot more.'

'Yeah, right,' Amy said with a smile.

In the days since she'd been rescued by her friends from the Terrible Teacake Tantrum (well, that's what they'd all called it ever since), Amy had been overwhelmed with help and support. She had an on-line counsellor now, and she'd had a long transatlantic phonecall from Ria. Amy knew both her weight and her BMI, she knew the acceptable limits, and she'd promised her friends and the school doctor to stay within those limits.

As a peace-offering, Niffy had asked her mum to contact her famous actress friend. She was sure Amy would take advice from Gwen Smith-Turner, because she was such a fan.

It had only taken a few days for an email – a real live, actual email – from the actress to drop into Amy's inbox.

My dearest Amy,
    How exciting to be performing in a school play at the end of term! I was in three plays at St J's, and I knew as soon as I stepped onto the school stage that I was going to make acting my career.
    It may sound silly, but when N-B

and I were at school, no one worried
about eating too much: everyone
worried about getting enough to eat.
We were always starving. All that
running around on the hockey pitch
every afternoon — not to mention
walking in and out of town — seemed
to keep us fit as fiddles.

It may sound plain and dreary when
there are so many diet books out
there telling you to stuff grapefruits
up your nose, eat only bacon or who
knows what other load of old rubbish,
but I still follow a diet which is
rather like the St Jude's one.

Three sensible meals a day, with
nothing in between. Well, maybe a
pot of plain yoghurt or a tiny bag
of peanuts if I'm absolutely
famished, but it's the exception
rather than the rule. Every thin
person I know eats like this. They
never, ever miss one single, boring
old meal. Breakfast, lunch and
dinner. Sensible food in moderation.
A little bit of pudding never hurt

anyone — and eat lots and lots of
vegetables. But not at breakfast! I
just won't do all that wacky kind of
thing. I have porridge and fruit, or
toast and an egg and a refreshing
cup of tea. Plain St Jude's fare.

Best dash up and down the hockey
pitch as much as you can —
apparently you're very good and
nearly made the Scottish team. To
have energy for that, my darling
girl, you need to eat!

Take care of your young and
beautiful self. Cherish your
friends, and for goodness' sake,
never, ever baste your lovely
complexion out in the sun. If
someone had told me that when I was
younger, I would have saved an
absolute bloody fortune on lotions,
potions, peels, creams, masks and
what have you. I'm sure you are
going to be simply wonderful in your
part. Break a leg!

All my very best wishes,
Gwen S-T

The letter had a strange effect on Amy. She'd laughed over it, then printed it out and shown it to lots of people who still didn't believe that someone so famous had actually written to her.

Best of all, Amy seemed to be following all the good advice she'd been given.

Breakfast was no longer a pained oatcake, devoid of any butter. And Gina was delighted to spot Amy back in the lunch queue, ordering ordinary helpings of main course; in the evenings, although she still steered clear of the four-o'clock cake buffet, she had supper with pudding just like everybody else.

She didn't look *fatter*. She just looked less gaunt and haunted. She had more energy, and her sparkly sense of fun and raucous laugh returned.

To make up for her part in the horrible row with Niffy, Amy also did something a little surprising. She wrote a long email of her own to Finn and explained how upset Niffy had been. Then, at the bottom of the letter, she set out her decision.

For now [she wrote to Finn], I think we should just be friends . . . I think that's what Niffy would prefer. Let's see what happens at Christmas. I'm going to come down for a weekend and

```
maybe we can talk. Don't have a go at
her about this, please. Let's just
all get on — that's what I want most.
    Lots of love,
    Amy x
```

She'd read it over several times and felt proud of herself. She really liked Finn, but in her heart she knew that Niffy's friendship was even more important to her.

'Your dress! It's recovered!' Amy exclaimed as soon as she set eyes on Gina.

Gina, Min and Niffy had decided to slip backstage twenty minutes before curtain up to wish Amy one final 'break a leg' and to see how good she looked in her stage make-up.

'I know,' Gina said, giving Amy a little twirl. 'Dermot's mum took it to a specialist cleaner and they managed to get every last bit of wine out.'

'Such a shame Dermot can't come tonight,' Niffy sighed, 'to see your masterpiece being performed.'

'I know.' Gina smiled shyly. 'But then I'm not sure I'd want him to know every little detail of how jealous I was about him ... I mean, I made lots of it up, obviously ...'

'We know,' Min reminded her with a wink.

A sixth former was still applying powder to Amy's face as she perched on a chair. 'Can't believe I'm going to be on stage in a school uniform,' Amy complained. 'Where is the glamour in that?! Couldn't you at least have put in a scene which called for a sparkly dress, Gina?'

'Sorry!' she apologized.

Peta came into the little backstage area, smiled a hello at everyone, then hurried over to take a look at Amy's face.

'Great job!' she said admiringly. 'You look so pretty.'

'You too – you look amazing,' Amy said generously, and of course she meant it – how could she not mean it? Peta was totally beautiful. She wore a ruffled scarlet dress, and her hair, curled into soft ringlets, looked almost transparently white.

'I have a present for you,' Peta said, and rummaged in her bag. She finally found a thin pink gauze bag, tied with pink ribbons. Inside it was a handful of dainty biscuits.

'Traditional Swedish,' Peta explained with a smile. 'For luck.'

'Thanks!' Amy said, accepting the gift and now feeling bad that she didn't have anything to give Peta. Not to mention hideously guilty that she had spent so much time disliking her.

'Has Finn wished you luck?' Niffy asked.

Amy nodded. Finn had accepted the 'friends' idea. But 'just till Christmas', he'd insisted.

'He wants to film me doing one of my speeches,' Amy told them.

'Better make him promise not to post it on YouTube,' Niffy warned.

'Wouldn't that be breaching Gina's copyright?' Min wondered.

'It's a great play, Gina,' Amy said proudly. 'Everyone's fussing over me, but it's Gina's play. She wrote it – she's so clever! Mrs Parker's going to call you up to take a bow with us at the end, by the way.'

'No!' Gina exclaimed, a little horrified, a little excited. 'Hey – we need to go and take our seats.'

'Break a leg!' they chorused to Amy one last time.

'What is this?' Peta asked in confusion. 'Everyone is telling me to break my leg? Why?'

When the lights went out, the curtain opened on Amy standing floodlit in the centre of the stage.

'Hi, Adrian . . . I'm so glad you could come . . .' she began in a voice which for a moment sounded both tight and wobbly, but as she went on, she began to breathe, to fill the space, to grow in confidence.

Gina, sitting in the darkness with her hands tightly clenched on her lap, felt almost as frightened as Amy, but as the words went on, filled out and became real once again, she too breathed a sigh of relief.

Then, for thirty-five minutes, three budding actors and one budding writer made a little very special magic. The magic which somehow, on an ordinary night, managed to transport an audience of four hundred fidgety, preoccupied school pupils and their teachers to somewhere completely new and different.

For thirty-five special minutes, they really did care about Stella and Adrian, and whether or not Scarlett was going to come between them. And when the curtain came down, Gina found herself clapping just as hard as everyone else in the audience, and brushing a tear from the corner of her eye.

Chapter Thirty-five

'We are not going to find anything here!' Amy protested in mock anger.

'Yes we are!' Greg insisted. 'We are probably going to find every single thing we could ever have wanted for Christmas, and much, much more besides.'

'C'mon,' Min said. Just a few moments ago, Greg had taken hold of her hand and now she was gripping it tightly, worried that if she accidentally let go, he would never hold her hand again. After the cinema disaster, she was determined to take every chance to get close to him today.

So Niffy and Amy followed Greg and Min into the huge discount store on Prince's Street.

It was the last Saturday of the autumn term, and every single boarder was out on the high street Christmas shopping.

It was a perfect shopping day. Cold and dark already, at three o'clock, with every street, every tree, every lamppost festooned with small, sparkling Christmas lights.

Yes, there were crowds, but they were cheery festive crowds; people who apologized and smiled when they bashed their bulging carrier bags against your legs. There was nothing but seasonal goodwill at the long queues for the tills.

The girls, on admittedly limited budgets, were buying presents for their families and friends. Min, who had far more brothers and sisters than anyone else, had much more shopping to do, and although Greg was supposed to be there to help, he was really only a distraction.

'Look!' Amy and Niffy said at exactly the same time, pointing at one of the tables laden with gifts – all the bits and bobs that wouldn't attract a glance at any other time of year.

The two girls raced each other to the table and snatched up the thing that had caught their eye at the same moment.

'I'm getting it for him!' Amy insisted.

'No, I am!' Niffy replied.

'I saw it first!'

'You did not!'

'For goodness' sake!' Min intervened.

Both Niffy and Amy had an old-fashioned film

clapperboard in their hands. Both knew that arty, film-making Finn would love it. Each one of his mini home films could now start with a call of 'Action!' and the snap of the clapperboard in front of the screen. He would be able to yell 'Cut!' and hear the satisfying snap.

'Maybe you could toss for it?' Min suggested.

'Stop it! Stop it, girls. Calm down,' Greg weighed in. 'It's OK – take the clapperboard, but over here I have found the gift that no man can be without. You will be fighting over who is going to give Finn this.' And he held up a mug which read: TOO SEXY FOR MY MUG.

'You have the board,' Niffy agreed straight away. 'I'm getting him that.'

'C'mon, fan out . . . shop, shop, shop – we should have left to meet Gina in the Arts Café' – Amy glanced at her watch – 'about twenty minutes ago.'

'Now you take a look at those.' Dermot handed a heavy plastic bag to Gina. 'I need to get up a ladder – very important job to do.'

He headed for the café entrance, which was filled with Christmas shoppers desperate for a seat and a caffeine fix, and began to set up a tall stepladder. As he went off in search of the toolbox, Gina unwrapped the package on her lap.

Inside the plastic bag were three rectangles swathed in bubble-wrap. Gina took out the first one and pulled off the Sellotape. She unwound the bubble-wrap until a framed photograph of an astonishingly white beach with blue sea slid out onto her lap. The small wooden fishing boat pulled up onto the sand was her clue that this was Barra rather than Barbados.

'Oh!' she said to herself. Dermot was so clever and so thoughtful! These were the pictures he'd promised to look out for her mother. And he'd had them framed! Opening the second and the third, she couldn't help but be impressed by how good they were. He was a really accomplished photographer.

She looked over at him, hoping to attract his attention and voice her thanks. But he was now halfway up the ladder, a hammer and what looked like a bush in one hand, several nails between his teeth and an expression of total concentration on his face.

Gina got up to take a closer look, and watched as Dermot reached up to nail a large ceiling hook in place. The nail wobbled a little and threatened to go in squint, but he was finally able to get the hook up.

Now he slid the huge bunch of greenery over the hook. He let go carefully, wanting to make sure it took the weight.

Everything seemed to be working: the green stems,

leaves and berries were dangling down in the doorway. It was enormous! Dermot's mother had gone totally over the top, as she tended to do at Christmas ('I'm a Christmas person – I like to pull out all the stops'). It went a little way to compensate for his dad's incredibly grumpy mood at this time of year. But then anything to do with spending money and having fun was bound to make his dad grumpy. Dermot glanced over towards the counter, where his dad was banging at the coffee machine, slamming down mugs and jugs and plates. In a hurry as usual. He shook his head. When was the guy ever going to lighten up?

'The photos are great!' Gina called up from the foot of the ladder. 'My mom is going to love them. It's really, really nice of you.'

'I'm a nice guy,' Dermot joked as he slowly made his way down the ladder. 'As long as your mom decides she can now love me, then my cunning plan will have worked.'

'What is that, by the way?' Gina pointed up at the enormous green bush.

'What is *that*?' Dermot asked in amazement. 'You don't know? I thought you guys invented it.'

'Huh?'

The café door opened, and Niffy and Amy burst in, followed by Greg and Min.

'Hi!' Dermot greeted them. 'I'm just explaining to Gina about mistletoe. Apparently she's never heard of it.'

'That's mistletoe?' Gina looked up in surprise. She'd never seen the real thing – well, if she had, she'd never seen so much of it. This was a great wild straggly bush, which Dermot's mother had hacked from an oak tree deep in a Borders forest.

'Yes!' Dermot told her. 'And there's a tradition – isn't there?' He looked over at Gina's friends for support.

'Oh yeah.' Gina smiled at him. 'I know all about the tradition.'

With that, she put her arms around Dermot's waist and, trying to forget that his dad was just across the room – not to mention many, many customers – closed her eyes and pulled him in for a kiss.

'Me too!' Niffy joked, and planted noisy, puckered smackers on both cheeks of the person standing next to her, which happened to be Amy.

'And you two!' Amy said, pointing at the slightly stunned Greg and Min. They were still holding hands and looking up at the mistletoe in some sort of reverential amazement.

Min turned to Greg.

Greg turned to Min.

She didn't dare close her eyes, because she didn't want anything unexpected to happen and put them off. Not this time.

No, this time it was definitely, definitely going to happen. Right now. She didn't care who was watching . . .

Right underneath the bush, Min and Greg stood and turned towards each other.

Greg's soft lips brushed against hers, and Min felt a thrill of surprise pass from her mouth to her toes. Just as she pressed her lips a little harder against Greg's, feeling the thrill pass from her toes and straight back up again, Dermot's bent nail pinged out of the plaster, the hook loosened, then jumped from the ceiling, sending the mistletoe crashing down on top of them.

'*Wow!*' was Dermot's response when the shrieks, shower of plaster dust and cries of surprise had died down. 'Now that's what I call chemistry!'

'No! *Physics!*' Min laughed.

MEET THE AUTHOR . . .

CARMEN

Full name: Carmen Maria Reid

Home: A creaky Victorian house
in Glasgow, Scotland

Likes: Writing (luckily), chocolate in any shape
or form especially if caramel is involved, Jack
Russell dogs, cute blue-eyed guys in glasses,
children (especially hers), buying handbags,
holidays by the sea, Earl Grey tea in
an insulated mug, very very long walks,
very, very long jeans, shepherd's pie,
hot bubble baths (for inspiration), duvet coats,
playing tennis

Dislikes: Large animals, drinking milk (bleurrrrgh),
high heels (she's already 6ft 1), going to the gym
(but she goes anyway), filling in forms or
paperwork of any kind, flying

Would like to be: The author of lots more books
(Secret ambition was to be a ballet dancer or
Olympic gold medal winning runner)

Fascinating fact: Carmen spent four years
boarding at a girls' school very like St J's

COMING SOON!

Read the brand-new St Jude's story.

Secrets at St Jude's: Rebel Girl
by Carmen Reid

At St Jude's School for Girls, four friends are facing
very different problems . . .

Can Gina still be happy with her boyfriend when
there's such an exciting new guy on the scene?

How will Amy survive when her rich dad's money disappears?

What can tomboy Niffy do to make herself gorgeous?

And why is Min spending so much time in the
study and missing all the fun?

Sounds like all the St Jude's friends need to get
in touch with their inner **Rebel Girl**!

Available June 2010 with a glamorous new cover look!

ISBN: 978 0 552 56122 8

Read about the St Jude's girls' first term together . . .

Secrets at St Jude's: New Girl
by Carmen Reid

Ohmigod! Gina's mum has finally flipped and is sending
her to Scotland to some crusty old boarding school called
St Jude's – just because Gina spent all her money on clothes
and got a few bad grades! It's so unfair!

Now the Californian mall-rat has to swap her sophisticated
life of pool parties and well-groomed boys for . . . hockey in
the rain, school dinners and stuffy housemistresses. And
what's with her three kooky dorm-buddies . . . could they ever
be her friends?

An addictive read
A hilarious read
A Carmen Reid

Available soon with a glamorous new cover look!

ISBN: 978 0 552 55706 1

Secrets at St Jude's: Jealous Girl
by Carmen Reid

Goodbye L.A., pools, malls and sunshine!

Hello Edinburgh, rain, hockey and school dinners!

Californian Gina is back in Scotland for a new term at
stuffy girls' school, St Jude's, and she's returned with
a secret jealousy.

But all the dorm girls have a reason to be jealous:
glamour-puss Amy is all green-eyed about Jason, swotty Min
longs to be like her cool friends and Niffy, stuck at home, is
jealous of everyone back at school.

The girls will have to stick together to make it
through this term!

Available soon with a glamorous new cover look!

ISBN: 978 0 552 55707 8